Debt Inheritance

INDEBTED #1

PEPPER WINTERS

Debt Inheritance (Indebted #1)
Copyright © 2014 Pepper Winters
Published by Pepper Winters

All rights reserved. No part of this book may be reproduced or transmitted in any form, including electronic or mechanical, without written permission from the publisher, except in the case of brief quotations embodied in critical articles or reviews.

This is a work of fiction. Names, characters, businesses, places, events, and incidents are either the products of the author's imagination or used in a fictitious manner. Any resemblance to actual persons, living or dead, or actual events is purely coincidental.

This book is licensed for your personal enjoyment only. This book may not be re-sold or given away to other people. If you would like to share this book with another person, please purchase an additional copy for each person you share it with. If you are reading this book and did not purchase it, or it was not purchased for your use only, then you should return it to the seller and purchase your own copy. Thank you for respecting the author's work.

Published: Pepper Winters 2014: **pepperwinters@gmail.com**
Cover Design: by Ari at Cover it! Designs:
http://salon.io/#coveritdesigns
Proofreading by: Jenny Sims:
http://www.editing4indies.com
Proofreading by: Kayla the Bibliophile:
https://www.facebook.com/KaylaTheBibliophile
Formatting by: http://www.blackfirefly.com/
Images in Manuscript from Canstock Photos:
http://www.canstockphoto.com

*For every reader, blogger, reviewer, and friend who made my dreams come true.
I write for you.
Forever.*

OTHER WORK BY PEPPER WINTERS

Pepper Winters is a New York Times, Wall Street Journal, and USA Today International Bestseller.

Her Dark Romance books include:
Monsters in the Dark Trilogy
Tears of Tess (Monsters in the Dark #1)
Quintessentially Q (Monsters in the Dark #2)
Twisted Together (Monsters in the Dark #3)

Indebted Series
Debt Inheritance (Indebted #1)
First Debt (Indebted Series #2)
Second Debt (Indebted Series #3)
Third Debt (Indebted Series #4)
Fourth Debt (Indebted Series #5)
Final Debt (Indebted Series #6)

Her Grey Romance books include:
Destroyed
Ruin & Rule (Pure Corruption MC #1)
Sin & Suffer (Pure Corruption MC #2)

Her Upcoming Releases include:
2016: Je Suis a Toi (Monsters in the Dark Novella)
January 2016: Sin & Suffer (Pure Corruption MC #2)
2016: Super Secret Series to be announced
2016: Unseen Messages (Standalone Romance)

Follow her on her website
Pepper Winters

This story isn't suitable for those who don't enjoy dark romance, uncomfortable situations, and dubious consent. It's sexy, it's twisty, there's colour as well as darkness, but it's a rollercoaster not a carrousel.

Warning heeded…enter the world of debts and payments.

(As an additional warning please note, this is a cliffhanger, answers will not be answered, the storyline won't be resolved, and character motivations won't be revealed until further on. It's a complex story that will unfold over a few volumes.)

If you would like to read this book with like-minded readers, and be in to win advance copies of other books in the series, along with Q&A sessions with Pepper Winters, please join the Facebook group below:

Indebted Series Group Read

Jethro

THE WORLD WAS a dangerous place, but I was worse.

The human race left the dark ages behind—technology improved and ruined our lives in equal measure, and the devils in society hid with better camouflage.

As the years rolled by, and we left our barbaric ways behind, people forgot about the shadows lurking in plain sight. Men like me morphed into predators in sheep's clothing. We preyed on the weak with no apology, and everything landed in our fucking laps. Civilization cloaked us, hiding the animals at heart.

We traded caveman mentality and murder for suits and softly spoken curses. I hid my true temper beneath a veil of decorum. I mastered the art of suave.

People who knew me said I was a gentleman. They called me distinguished, accomplished, and shrewd.

I was all of those things, but none of them. We might live in a civilized world, but rules and laws didn't apply to me. I was a rule-breaker, curse-maker, life-stealer.

The projection was a farce—but even the worst of us had someone who owned us. Whether family, honour, or duty.

I'd embraced my inner barbarian, yet was governed by a hierarchy and when the Hawk matriarch snapped her fingers,

we all came running.
    Including my arsehole of a father, Bryan Hawk.
    There, in the cigar and cognac laced library, I learned a truth that forever changed my life.
    And *hers*.
    My family owned another.
    An IOU on their entire existence.
    Who gave a shit why a wealthy family called the Weavers were indebted to us? Who gave a damn that they'd royally fucked off my family and earned the wrath of my ancestors?
    All I cared about was the news I'd inherited something more than just money, possessions, or titles.
    My twenty-ninth birthday gave me a pet. A toy.
    A responsibility I didn't want.
    Debts I had to extract from unwilling flesh.
    A job to uphold our family honour.
    Nila Weaver.
    One mistake six hundred years ago put a curse on her entire family.
    One mistake sold her life to me in a mountain of unpayable debt.
    I inherited her.
    I preyed on her.
    I owned her life and had the piece of paper to prove it.
    Nila Weaver.
    Mine.
    And my task…
    …
    …
    devour her.

"TOLD YOU THIS collection would be your break, Threads."

I smiled, not taking my eyes off the model prancing down the runway. My stomach churned like an overworked loom with stress and adrenaline.

"Don't jinx it. There's still the couture collection to go." I flinched as the model sashayed too much, wobbling in the insanely high heels I'd buckled to her feet.

My cell-phone buzzed in the only place I had available in this dress—my cleavage.

No, no. Not now.

I'd been waiting to hear from him for two days. Lying in bed in the fancy hotel, willing my phone to chime, granting me the intoxicating rush of flirtation. But nothing. Not a peep.

A month of this…*what was this?* It wasn't a relationship. Liaison? Nameless courtship? I had no name for the craziness I indulged in. I panted for scraps of communication like a high-school wallflower.

It's time to end it.

Another message vibrated, shattering my willpower to ignore him with his impeccable timing—as usual.

"You know the couture line will raise the roof. Stop being

modest." Vaughn nudged my shoulder with his.

Ignoring my brother and the suddenly heavy cell-phone, I winced as the model flicked her hair pirouetting at the end of the runway, before flouncing away in a whirl of pink silk.

Too much attitude for that dress. I shook my head, stopping the inner monologue that never shut up when it came to models flaunting my creations.

"I don't know anything anymore. Stop nettling me, V. Let me focus."

Vaughn scowled. "I don't know why you're so worried. Cheque books are already open. You'll see."

Another message arrived, sending my phone into throbbing excitement. Even my phone got excited when he texted.

My heart fluttered. A hot flush covered my body remembering the last sentence I'd received from Kite007. I'd made the mistake of reading it just as I boarded the short flight from England to Spain.

Kite007: *I don't need to know what you look like to get hard—guess where my hand is.*

Of course I couldn't help myself. Because I was a sex-starved woman surrounded by over-protective men.

I replied: *I don't need to hear what you sound like to get wet—guess where my hand wants to be?*

I'd never been so blatant. With anyone. The moment I sent it I freaked out, wishing I could unsend.

I'd spent the trip in a confused state of arousal and denial. And never received a reply.

Until now.

I hid my flush, pretending nothing enticing taunted me on my phone. I loved my father and brother—so damn much—but if they knew...the proverbial shit would hit the fan.

"Oh, God." I clutched my heart as another stick-thin model paraded down the catwalk, failing to show off the intricate peacock-blue dress to its advantage. "No one will buy it if they can't see the potential of the design."

Vaughn sighed. "You worry too much. It's stunning. Anyone can see that." His dark eyes landed on mine. "Allow a thrill of pride—just once, Threads. It's going perfectly, and I couldn't be prouder of you." My twin brother draped his arm over my shoulders, tucking me against him. Considering the word 'twin' meant mirror image, Vaughn was taller, better looking, and overall more vibrant than me. He made others envious with his natural beauty, while I made others feel beautiful with dresses sewn with twenty-four carat gold and dyed with exclusive inks costing a small fortune.

I supposed that was my talent: making others feel worthy while he sold products thanks to his allure. Mirror image alright—the direct opposite.

"You're a model. Why aren't you showcasing my clothes?"

Vaughn laughed. "My figure doesn't look good squashed into some sequinned frock. Create some decent clothes for males, then I might stoop and be your headline act."

I thumped his arm. "You know I don't have the drive to stitch suits and boxer-shorts. I keep telling you to go into business with me and create a men's line. There'd be no stopping—"

Vaughn rolled his eyes. "Can't afford me."

I scowled. "Afford you? I've heard a perky pair of boobs and sex will buy your attention for at least a weekend."

He pointed at my small chest with a glint in his eye. "I see no perky pair and…gross, Nila. You're my sister. Why the hell are we talking about sex? You know we were raised better than that."

I didn't want to laugh. I didn't want to lose the wound-up tension from my collection, but Vaughn never failed to earn a lip-twitch.

I sighed, shaking my head. "Sex, shmex. You'd be lucky if I hired your scrawny ass."

He smirked. "Who're you calling scrawny?" He waved at his tall frame. "My skills are on the other end of the camera. As my track record states." His perfectly straight teeth flashed—

daring anyone to deny the truth.

I used to be jealous of his deliciously good looks. My brother was rich brocade while I was boring calico. But now, I was proud. I might be graced with a body requiring embellishment by other means than fate, but I knew the secrets of illusion. I'd spun magic with a sewing machine since I was a little girl, stepping from the shadow of my family's name, carving a small slice of greatness for myself.

"Well if the show tonight flops, at least you can bail me out with all that cash you've earned thanks to your god-like looks."

A laugh barrelled from his mouth, loud but still hidden by the sultry fashion show music. The dark room hid the large crowd but couldn't disguise the heavy press and body heat of numerous buyers, shoppers, and catalogue procurers.

Vaughn squeezed me tighter. "Nila, I'm warning you. I want a smile. You've worked on this for months. Stop being so damn pessimistic and celebrate."

"I can't celebrate until the last model has shown their garment and not tripped over their arse in a seven thousand dollar dress."

My phone buzzed again.

I froze, cursing my twisting stomach and the fire-bolt to my core. Kite007. The nameless teasing male who had more power over me than any other man. A stupid secret crush. With a stranger no less.

It's a sad day when I'm emotionally invested in a fantasy. I should never have replied to the incorrectly sent message a month ago. Then I might've directed the small energy I had left after working so hard and find a real man. One I could kiss and flirt with in person.

The jagged pain lashed again. Rejection. I'd asked Kite, after a late night volley of messages, if he'd be interested in meeting.

Needle&Thread: *So…I was wondering…I'm sitting here drinking a glass of wine and thought you might like to do that sometime?*

Go out for a drink, in person, together?

I'd pressed send on the jumbled, awkward sentence before I lost my nerve. I'd never asked anyone on a date before—it nearly gave me a heart attack.

He'd never replied. Silence was his usual reaction to dealing with something he didn't want to discuss—only to message a few days later on a completely different subject.

Where sexual innuendoes were hard for me, Kite007 was a master. He used it as a weapon, making me forget we had no depth to our conversations...not that they *were* conversations.

When he did reply, it'd been a clever mix of teasing and emptiness—reminding me not to read into this shallow form of communication.

Kite007: *I'm in a meeting and all I can think about is your nun outfit. You wearing underwear today?*

Yep. That stopped my wishful thinking of meeting him in person.

Untangling myself from Vaughn, I pretended to scrutinize the remaining models while I indulged in the very first text I received.

The one that began it all.

Kite007: *Tonight won't work for me, but waiting will only make you wetter. Be a good girl and don't argue. I'll make sure to reward your patience.*

A shiver worked its way under my expensive gown. I'd never received a message like that. Ever. And it wasn't meant for me. I imagined some lucky woman looking forward to her reward. I tried to delete the message—I really did. But after twenty-four years of being hidden away from boys, I couldn't help myself.

My reply was utterly ridiculous.

Needle&Thread: *I'm afraid you're talking to a nun who understands nothing of sexual hints and not-so-subtle suggestions. Patience to me is payment after waiting for a microwaved chocolate pudding. Wet to me is the brief enjoyment of a shower before the slave labour of my job. If your intention was to make me (an unknown stranger who could be your mother-in-law or an arthritic eighty-year-old) wet and impatient, perhaps you could bribe me with sugar, a hot bath, and a night off from work— then perhaps I'll obey and 'deserve' your veiled insinuation of pleasure. (By the way…if you haven't guessed, wrong number.)*

And so began a mistake that I had no intention of stopping.

I groaned under my breath, never failing to suffer a wash of embarrassment. I had no idea where the flippancy came from. I wasn't a nun—but I wasn't far off. Thanks to the two permanent men in my life, dating was a rare event.

A curvy model coasted down the runway in my favourite creation of cream lace, Victorian collar, and external bustle. I intended to head the trend of a historical fashion comeback.

"That would look better on you." Vaughn's husky voice cut through the graceful music.

I shook my head. "No chance." Looking down at my small cup size and overly trim frame, thanks to my obsessive running, I added, "You need femininity to pull off a corset like that. I'm a rake."

"Only because you exercise too damn much."

Only because I have you and father stopping me from getting exercise in sexual form. I didn't believe in self-pleasuring…running was my only hope at a release.

The model spun in place, swirling her train before disappearing up the catwalk. I suffered a moment of envy. It would be nice to have boobs and hips.

Vaughn's strong fingers caught my chin, breaking the unlockable stare I had on the strutting model, guiding my nondescript black eyes to his vibrant chocolate ones. "We're going out tonight. Hitting the Milan night clubs." The low lights around the runway made his skin glow with a natural dusky tan. His blue-black hair was the one beautiful thing I shared. Thick, dead straight, and so glossy people said it was like looking into black glass.

My one saving grace.

Oh, and my ability to sew.

And flirt with a stranger on an impersonal device.

My phone buzzed—a reminder my inbox had something delicious for me to read. And it would be delicious.

Dammit. The urge to look almost broke my self-control. What the hell was he doing messaging me? We knew nothing about each other. We shared nothing but dirty fantasies. My mind once again jumped back to the first relay of texts.

Kite007: *Shit, you're a nun? Sorry…what's the correct term of address…sister? I apologise for the incorrectly sent message. Despite your Godly perfection and sheltering, you deduced correctly. It was in fact very sexual. The woman in mind would never be welcomed into a sanctity such as yours.*

I'd had no reply to that, but he'd sent another twenty minutes later.

Kite007: *Sister…I need absolution. I find myself consumed with the image of a sexy nun stripping and sliding into a hot bath with chocolate sauce on her lips. Does that make me the devil, or are you for making me lust for someone I shouldn't?*

For the first time in my life, I'd felt the rush of power and need. This unknown man lusted for me. He'd replied based on what I'd sent. He'd been right about the blushing, but only because I was sheltered, not because I'd decided to dress in black and white garb for the rest of my life. I came from rainbow fabric; I drank textile ink as mothers' milk. I learned to sew before I could walk. I could never become a nun, purely because of the boring fashion choices.

My fingers shook as I messaged him back.

Needle&Thread: *I'm blushing but happen to be wearing something a lot more interesting than black and white or a boring shift.*

I had no idea what made me reply. I'd never been so bold and he was taken—obviously. He'd been messaging a girl.

Kite007: *Oh, see…you can't say things like that to a complete stranger who mistakenly messaged a hot nun who doesn't conform to the dress code picked out by God. Tell me.*

Needle&Thread: *Tell you what?*

Kite007: *What are you wearing?*

And that was where I freaked. He could be a ninety-year-old pervert who'd tracked down my number from one of my runway shows to stalk me. Nothing was as it seemed in today's world.

Needle&Thread: *I hope you find the person you were trying to contact. Enjoy your night of sexual torture. Goodbye.*

I'd closed my phone and done exactly what I'd said. Microwaved a chocolate pudding and slid into a hot bath. Only to be interrupted by a reply.

And another.

And another.

I lost count of how many messages I received. I managed to ignore him for five hours, but then my innocent soul became corrupted by a man I'd never met.

"What do you say?" Vaughn pursed his lips, accenting his well-formed jaw and rounded cheekbones.

I blinked, shattering memories of phone flirting.

"Huh?"

"Tonight. You. Me. A bottle of tequila and some bad decisions." My brother rolled his eyes. "I'm not having you holed away in your hotel room on your own—not after a show like this." Vaughn's voice cajoled, his face—a cross between a cherub-faced youth and heartbreaker man—implored. I could never say no to him. Just like countless other women. It didn't help he was heir to a textile business that'd been in our family since the thirteenth century and a seriously good catch.

We had pedigree.

History.

The bond between past and present. Dreams and requirements. Freedom and obligation. We had plenty of it, and the weight of what was expected of me hammered me further and further into the ground.

"No tequila. No night clubs. Let me unwind in peace. I need some quiet after the hectic day I've had."

"All the more to get messy on a dance floor." Vaughn grabbed my elbow, attempting to swing me around in a complicated dance move.

I stumbled. "Get your grubby hands off me, V." Vaughn was the only one who didn't inherit a nickname based on the industry that consumed not only our lives but our ancestors, too.

"That's no way to speak to your brother, Threads." V laughed.

"What's this? My two offspring fighting?"

I rolled my eyes as the distinguished silhouette of my father appeared from the crowd of buyers, designers, and movie starlets all there to witness the new season of fashion in Milan. His dark brown eyes crinkled as he smiled. "Congratulations, sweetheart."

Vaughn let me go, relinquishing his sibling hug for a paternal squeeze. My arms slinked around the toned middle of my father. Archibald Weaver still had the Weaver signature thick black hair with a straight spine, sharp mind, and ruggedly handsome face. He only became more fetching the older he got.

"Hey. I didn't think you'd arrive in time." Pulling away, I inhaled his strong cologne. I wished mum was still around to see him evolve from distracted parent to fantastic support system. I never knew why we weren't close when I was young. He'd been sour, grumpy, and…lost. But he'd never burdened Vaughn or me with what troubled him. He remained a strict single parent, raising us motherless from eleven years old.

"I managed to get an earlier flight. Couldn't miss your headline show."

Another message came through, the vibration particularly violent. I shuddered and blocked all thoughts of the nameless man trying to get my attention.

"I'm glad. However, all you're going to see is your daughter shuffle down the runway, overshadowed by gorgeous models, and then trip off the end."

My father laughed, his critical eye perusing my gown. "Corset, tulle, and the new midnight-galaxy material—I doubt anyone will overshadow you."

"Help me convince her to join me tonight. We could all go out together," Vaughn said.

Great. Another night with two men—neither of whom I can avoid to acquire a real relationship.

I often felt like a kitten brought up by two tigers. They never let me grow up. Never permitted my own claws to form or teeth to sharpen.

My father nodded. "Your brother is right. It's been a few months since we were together. Let's make a night of it. Some of your best work is on display. You've made me very proud, Nila, and it's time to celebrate."

I sighed. Looking over his shoulder, I saw the last model disappearing into the wings, her train of silver stars and organza looking as if she'd fallen from heaven.

That's my cue.

"Fine. Sounds wonderful. I can never say no to you. Let me wrap this up and then I'll relax. Promise." I reached up and kissed him on his papery cheek. "Keep your fingers crossed that I don't trip and ruin my career."

He grinned, slipping into the much loved and well known persona of Tex—short for Textile—a nickname he'd had all my life.

"You don't need luck. Knock 'em dead." His brown eyes faded. The melancholy I was so used to seeing swallowed him whole, hiding his jovial spirit. It was his curse. Ours. All of us.

Ever since mum divorced him and disappeared we'd never been the same.

Vaughn pecked my cheek. "I'll help you get through the crowd."

I nodded and weaved through the crush of bodies to the small staircase at the side of the runway.

The organiser, with her headset, frantic blonde curls, and dog-eared notebook, squealed when her eyes landed on mine. "Ah! I'd sent out ninjas to find you. You're up. Like right now."

Vaughn chuckled. "I'll wait here for you." He faded into the living organism that was the fashion hungry crowd, leaving me at the mercy of Blonde Curls.

Bunching the overflowing train of my dress, I climbed the steps, hoping against all odds that I wouldn't faint. "Yes. I know. That's why I'm here."

"Thank God. Okay, stand there." She manhandled me until I stood just so. "I'll give you the cue in thirty seconds."

The girl couldn't have been much younger than me. I'd just celebrated my twenty-fourth birthday, but after leaving school at sixteen to follow in my family's footsteps and nurture my skills as a designer, I felt much older, grumpier, and less eager to please.

I love my job. I love my job.

And it was true. I *did* love my job. I loved transforming plain fabric, sourced by my father, into works of art thanks to the accessories, silks, and diamantes my brother imported when he wasn't modelling. We were a true family business. Which I loved and would never change.

It was the public eye I hated. I'd always been a homebody. Partly out of choice—partly because my father never let me date.

Talking of dates…

My fingers itched to grab my phone.

The girl nodded, pressing her headset hard to her ear. "Gotcha. Sending on now." Holding her hand out, she added, "Come. Your final model is ready. Get onto the runway."

I nodded, gathering the thick black material of the feather and gemstone dress I wore. Completely impractical. Completely couture. A bloody nightmare to wear, but the effect of soft wispy feathers and the glint of black diamantes set my hair off better than any other colour.

Some said colour was what made your mood.

I said black protects.

It gave me strength and boldness where I had none. It granted sexuality to a woman who'd been sheltered all her life by a severely overprotective father and insanely possessive brother.

If it hadn't been for Darren and the one night where I'd drunk too much, I would still be a virgin.

Taking my place in the middle of the runway, I smiled tightly at the model chosen to wear my centrepiece.

My heart fluttered, falling in love—just like I always did—with the garment I'd adoringly, intimately created. Wrapped around the girl's zero-size frame and shimmering in the low lights of the packed room, the dress was revolutionary. My career would reach new heights. It wasn't pride glowing in my heart—it was relief. Relief that I hadn't let anyone down—including myself.

I'd done it.

Despite my nerves, I'd done what I'd always needed and carved a name for myself despite the huge inheritance of the Weaver name and empire.

My collection was mine.

Every item from handbags to shoes and scarfs was mine. *Nila.*

Just my first name. I hadn't wanted to use the power of our legacy. I hadn't wanted to let anyone down in case I failed. But now I wanted to sequester my success and hoard it.

The room hushed with anticipation as the music changed from Latin to symphony. A large spotlight drenched us in golden rays.

My heart rate exploded as I took the model's hand, flashing her a quick smile. Her cascading blonde hair glittered with gold plaited in the strands.

We matched perfectly in height—deliberately placed together for ultimate impact. Gliding forward in thousand dollar shoes, we walked the final stretch.

My black ensemble set off the gold, yellow, and burnt orange of her layers upon layers. She looked like crackling embers and fire where I was the coal from which she sprang. We were the sunset of the show. The darlings of Milan.

Hushed silence. Bright lights. Immense concentration to stay on my feet.

The rest became a blur. There were no trips, or wobbles, or rushes of horror. Cameras clicked, praise murmured, and then it was over.

A year of hard work wrapped up in a two hour runway show.

The end of the platform became a sea of petals and strewn flowers full of accolades. Our coal and fire presence swallowed camera flashes, welcoming greedy eyes to stare.

Ten minutes I stood and drowned in praise. Vertigo hobbled my body as my gaze landed on my father and brother. They knew this part was the hardest for me. They knew my heart strummed fast and sickness rolled. Stress never sat well with my system.

Vertigo was hard to diagnose, but moments like these—where the madness of the past year culminated with yet more deadlines on the horizon—I recognised every symptom of wobbliness and fading vision. I felt drunk…I *wanted* to be drunk—even though I hadn't had liquor in seven years.

Swallowing the lightheadedness, I waved and bowed before hitting my limit. Gritting my teeth, I almost fell down the steps at the front of the runway right into Vaughn's arms.

He scooped me up, giving me a firm balanced form to clutch to. "Breathe through it. It'll pass."

Shaking my head, I blinked, chasing away the fear in my blood and weakness of an incurable illness. "I'm okay. Just let me go for a second."

He did as I asked, giving me space. The crowd stayed behind their small barricade letting me suck in much needed oxygen. My phone buzzed again and this time…I couldn't ignore it.

Pulling it from my ruffled, feathered cleavage, I unlocked the screen and indulged.

Kite007: *Haven't had a message from you in a couple of days. If you don't send one immediately, I might have to track down your name and location and come and spank you.*

My stomach flipped at the threat. He'd never insinuated a meeting...not after my bungle of asking him out and his blatant refusal.

Kite007: *Still no reply. If threats of physical harm won't make you respond, perhaps the mental visualisation of me stroking myself while reading some of your old messages will persuade you to.*

My core clenched. He'd pleasured himself while thinking of me? A stranger touching himself shouldn't give me such a thrill.

Kite007: *My Naughty Nun, I don't know what you're doing, but I've disgraced myself by coming all over my hand at the thought of you naked and smeared in chocolate. Hope you're happy.*

"What are you reading?" Vaughn peered over my shoulder.

My cheeks flamed and I wiped the screen of evidence that despite his and my father's best intentions, I'd managed to find a man interested in talking sex with me. I couldn't wait to be in private to respond. Kite seemed more...open. Maybe we could talk about real things and not just dirt.

"Nothing."

Vaughn scowled, then a large grin brightened his face. "Guess how many orders?"

My brain couldn't switch from wanting desperately to respond to Kite to normal conversation. "Orders?"

He threw his hands up. "Seriously! Your collection. Sometimes I worry about you, Threads." Still grinning, he added, "Your Fire and Coal collection has orders from all major retail chains in Europe and America, and the couture line is currently in a bidding war for exclusivity between a London boutique and Paris." He bounced with happiness—infecting me with energy. "I told you this was your break. You've cemented your name. *Nila* will be worn by celebrities around the world at their red-carpet premieres."

He lowered his voice. "You're your own, sister. You're more than just a Weaver. You're *you*, and I'm so damn proud of what you've achieved." Twin intuition had always been strong—showing just how much he understood without me ever having to voice it.

Tears sprang to my eyes. Vaughn didn't get sentimental often, so his praise was a well-placed dagger in my self-control. This time I couldn't stop the smile breaking through my defences or my heart glowing with accomplishment. "Thank you, V. That means—"

"Nila."

I spun around to face my father. Instead of the grin and look of love I expected, he stood cold and fierce. My stomach tensed, sensing something was wrong. So, so wrong. It was the same look he got whenever he thought of Mum. The same look I'd grown accustomed to hating and running from.

"Dad…what—" He wasn't alone. My eyes trailed from my father's pressed tux toward the tall, svelte man beside him.

Holy hell, who on earth…

Thoughts died like windless kites, littering my mind with silent dumbness. He was a stranger. But I felt as if I'd seen him before. He was a mystery. But I sensed I already knew everything about him. Two extremes…two confusions.

"Nila, I want to introduce you to someone." My father's jaw ticked, hands clenching into white-knuckled fists. "This is Jethro Hawk. He's a big fan of your work and would like to take you out tonight to celebrate your success."

I wanted to rub my eyes and have my hearing checked. Since the day of my birth, my father had never introduced me to a man. *Never.* And he'd never lied so obviously. This man wasn't a fan of my work—although he did have incredible fashion sense. He had to be a male model with his height, envious cheekbones, and perfectly styled salt-and-pepper hair. His white skin was flawless—no wrinkles or blemishes. He looked ageless, but I guessed he was late twenties despite his greying hair speaking of wisdom far beyond his years.

His hands were concealed in pockets of a dark charcoal suit with a cream shirt open at the throat and a diamond pin piercing his jacket lapel.

"Tex, what are you—" Vaughn's voice was quiet but possessive. Eyeing up Jethro, he stayed polite by offering his hand. "Nice to meet you, Mr. Hawk. I appreciate your interest in my sister's talent, but my father has it wrong. Tonight she is unavailable due to a family commitment."

I would've smiled if my stomach wasn't knotted as the two men assessed each other.

Jethro slowly took my brother's hand, shaking once. "Pleasure, I'm sure. And I, in turn, can appreciate your interest in keeping your prior agreement with your sister, but alas. Your generous father has allowed me the enjoyment of ruining your plans and stealing her away." His voice whispered through my gown, sending goosebumps down my spine. His accent was English, same as mine, but slightly more clipped. He sounded posh but rogue at the same time. Refined but uncouth.

My brother wasn't impressed. His forehead furrowed.

"I hope that isn't going to be an issue, Mr. Weaver. I've heard a lot about you and your family and would hate to upset you." Mr. Hawk's eyes landed on mine, capturing me in a cage of golden irises and effortless power. "However, I've heard the most about your sister. And I have no doubt it will be a pleasure knowing her."

I gulped. No one had spoken to me like that—especially in front of my *father*. Who was this man? Why did his very existence fill me with hot and cold and awareness and fear?

"Listen here," my father blustered. I tensed, ready for the outrage I knew he was capable of, but his lips snapped closed and the fire in his gaze didn't erupt. Swallowing hard, he finished, "I presume my obligations are complete?"

Jethro nodded, a lock of hair brushing his forehead. "You presume correctly."

Fear evolved to panic. Obligations? *My God, is my father in some sort of trouble?* I clutched his sleeve. "Dad. The show's over. Let's go for that drink." I glanced at Vaughn, cursing my fluttering heart and the mix-match of emotions colliding inside.

My father pulled me close, pressing a single kiss on my cheek. "I love you, Nila, but I've kept you to myself for long enough. Mr. Hawk has asked if he can take you out tonight. I agreed. Vaughn and I can wait till another time."

He didn't say—*only if you want to, of course*. It sounded more like a sentencing rather than freedom to date. Why this man? Why now?

Vaughn moved closer. "Tex, we already had plans. We can't just—"

My father glared at my brother, his gaze weighty with unsaid anger. "Plans change, V. Now give your sister a kiss goodbye. She's leaving."

"I am?" I took a step backward, clutching my phone. There was no denying Jethro Hawk was good looking and seemed to be successful judging by his attire, but if I was allowed to date, I wanted Kite007, not this cold outlander.

"You are." Jethro held out his hand, his gaze noosing me tighter in their golden cage. "I'm taking you somewhere special."

"She isn't going anywhere with you unless she wants to, dickhead." Vaughn puffed out his chest, placing a hand on my lower back. "Tex—tell him."

My eyes flew to my father. What existed in his gaze sent frost crackling through my blood. His lips were tight, eyes bright and slightly glassy. But his cheeks were dark with rage. He glowered at Mr. Hawk. "I've changed my mind. Not tonight."

Vaughn huffed, nodding in agreement. The thick soup of male testosterone choked my lungs.

Jethro smiled coolly. "You've given me your word, Mr. Weaver. There are no rain checks." Aiming his sharp smile my way, he purred, "Besides, Ms. Weaver and I have a lot to discuss. It's time we got acquainted and tonight is the night."

"Excuse me while you all fight over me. But what about what I want?" I crossed my arms. "I'm tired, overworked, and not in the mood to entertain. Thank you for your interest, but—"

"No buts, Ms. Weaver. It's been arranged and discussed. You will come with me because it's the only way your night will end." Jethro lowered his head, watching me from beneath his brow. "I promise you'll have a good time. And I mean you no harm...do you really think your father would permit me to take you out otherwise?"

Coldness etched his gaze.

Aloofness whispered from his posture.

Calculation radiated from his every pore.

I'd never been so intimidated or so intimately challenged.

My father might have permitted this, but he didn't condone it. Somehow Jethro had achieved the unachievable and convinced my father he was dateable material. If he could manipulate Archibald 'Tex' Weaver, I didn't stand a chance...and yet...despite the arrogance and chilly façade, he intrigued me.

My father had kept me captive my whole life. This was the first man to stand up to him and grant a glimmer of freedom.

The fear disappeared, leaving a flicker of interest. If this was the only man I could spend an evening alone with, I would take it. I would practice my non-existent flirting skills and grow my confidence so I could ask Kite007 out again. And next time, I wouldn't take no for an answer.

Sucking in a gulp, I placed my hand gently into Mr. Hawk's. His touch was as cold as his demeanour and just as strong. I froze as his fingers tightened around mine, tugging me forward. "Good decision, Ms. Weaver. I look forward to getting to know you better."

My lungs dragged in his scent of leather and woods. Words deserted me.

The show disappeared along with my worry and thoughts of Kite007. Gone was the urge to return to an empty hotel room. This man was pure danger, and I'd never sampled anything but safety. "And you, Mr. Hawk," I murmured.

My date smiled, transforming his face from handsome to

ruthless. "Please, call me Jethro." Changing our grip from handshake to handhold, he pulled me forward—away from my family, away from the men I'd known all my life, and toward a future I had no understanding of.

Vaughn's hand fell from my lower back.

I didn't look back.

I should've looked back.

I should never have placed my hand into that of a monster's.

That was the last day of freedom. The last day that was my own.

Individuality and uniqueness—those two words were so precious once upon a time. I'd been brought up with a gruff but fair father and a brother who I would marry if it wasn't incest, believing I was unique, different, never before created.

I hated being lied to.

I hated even more believing those lies until the truth decided to come for me.

Turned out, I was never an individual; I was a possession to trade.

I was never unique; someone had lived my life many times before, never free, never whole.

My life was never mine.

My destiny was already written.

My story began the night he came for me.

Jethro

IT WAS TOO easy.

I'd stolen her right before her father and brother. I'd taken her with no blood shed or bones broken.

Power wasn't threats or uncivilised fighting. It wasn't brawn or hard-won arguments.

Power was holding something so absolute, a man would do what he was told—all the while cursing your very soul. True power wasn't wielded by gangs or even loudly-spoken governments.

True power. *Limitless* power—only graced a fair few. It gave those lucky ones the ability—the nobility, to be courteous and polite. All while holding their fucking balls in their hands.

Archibald Weaver was one such example.

I shook my head, disbelieving how the so-called enemy of my family handed over his only daughter. The same daughter I'd seen in tabloids as a rising star of designers. The same offspring who was never photographed with a man on her arm or seen sneaking out of a restaurant with a hidden lover. He'd wanted to kill me. I had no doubt he would *try* to kill me.

But he would fail.

Just like he failed to protect her.

Because he had no fucking power.

All it had taken was two sentences and Nila went from his to mine. A thrill ran down my spine, remembering the rush of sensation when I'd tapped him on the shoulder. His dark eyes had been cool but welcoming, believing I was a stranger there to congratulate. That all changed when I handed over a black-flocked business card and said, "The time is nigh to pay your debts. Your past has found you, and there will be no peace until she's ours."

His eyes went from cool to glinting with horror and rebellion. He knew everything I did. He knew there was only one thing he could do—no matter that it would break his heart.

This was his fate. Her fate. *Their* fate. It'd been written and understood the moment he'd knocked up his wife.

He knew the consequences, and he also knew the power we controlled. No matter his unwillingness and terror, there was no other course of action.

Without a single word, he'd marched me to his daughter and placed her life in my hands. I hadn't believed my father when he said it would go so smoothly. After all—none of this made sense. But it had. And it did. And now…it was all on me.

My education had begun a month ago. I'd been told of my upcoming duties, given history lessons of past debt collections. But I was as new to this as her.

We came from generations interlocked in the same untieable way.

Now, it was our turn.

And we would have to learn together.

I glared at my conquest. Letting her hand go, she glided beside me wrapped in darkness. I didn't need a physical claim on her now that she was outside—alone. Was it trust in her father's judgement guiding her feet or stupidity?

Either way, I would be the last person she would ever see.

Nila

I BREATHED A lungful of crisp Milan air as we left the ornate building where the fashion show was held. For late summer, the temperature danced with chill rather than heat. The night had finally claimed the day. It didn't get dark until ten p.m., so it was late for me. This time of evening, I would normally be buried under a mound of cotton with a chalk pen and scissors deciding what my next creation would be.

Coldness darted through my blood—not from the cool breeze but from *him*. The silent, foreboding man walking soundlessly beside me.

Who is he? And why don't I trust a thing about him?

Studying him in my peripheral vision, he seemed to give off two personas. One, a cordial, well-dressed gentleman who looked as though he'd stepped through a wormhole from some ancient century. And two, an assassin who moved like a dancer only because he'd been taught the art of war and murder from the crib.

No words were spoken. No dalliance or small talk. His silence was strangely welcomed and hated. Welcomed because it meant I could focus on my vertigo and not let stress topple me over, hated because I wanted to *know* him. I wanted to know why my father had vouched for him and just where the hell he was taking me.

"I don't believe you," I said, my voice slicing through the crisp evening.

Even in the gloom, with only street lights for illumination, his eyes were bright and such a light brown they seemed otherworldly. His eyebrow rose, but no other interest showed on his face. "What don't you believe?" He fanned his arm to the left, indicating for me to travel that way.

My feet behaved, tottering obediently in the black velvet heels, but my brain swam with a sudden gyroscope of vertigo. I focused hard on the diamond glinting on Jethro's lapel. *Find an anchor. Hold on tight. Do this and you'll be alright.* The stupid rhyme echoed in my brain. My brother had made it up when we were eight after I'd broken my arm falling off the bottom step of our porch.

"That you convinced my father that you're dateable material." I bunched the front of my skirt, wishing I could've changed before traipsing through Milan in a couture dress. "You either bribed him or threatened."

Just like you're threatening me with your silence and imposing attributes.

"Threatened….interesting word." His voice positively purred. Placing his hands into his pockets, he added, "And if I did? What difference does it make? You're still here—with me—alone. Dangerous, really."

The footpath decided to roll beneath my suddenly unsure feet. *Breathe. Get it together.*

Heroines in books were portrayed as quaint and lovable if they were clumsy. I had more bruises and scrapes from falling and slamming into things than I would ever admit, and there was nothing quaint about it. I was a hazard. Especially if I had a pair of wickedly sharp dress scissors in my hands and stood up too fast. Anyone in a two metre radius was in danger if my brain decided to throw me helter-skelter into a wall.

It was also a huge inconvenience when faced with an overbearing stranger who just used the words *alone* and *dangerous*.

"Dangerous isn't a good word," I muttered, allowing a little physical distance to grow between us.

"Stupid isn't a good word either, but it's been echoing in my head."

I slammed to a halt. "Stupid?"

Jethro glided to a stop, looking so cultured and sharp I had a terrible urge to rip his jacket or ruffle his hair. He was too perfect. Too collected. Too *restrained.* My heart stuttered. *What exactly is he restraining?*

"You say I threatened your father as there's no other explanation as to why you're standing here with me. I say if you feel that way, then you're stupid for agreeing. It was *you* who took my hand, you who followed me from the crowd to empty streets." Leaning down, his eyes narrowed. "Stupid, Ms. Weaver. Very stupid indeed."

I should've been insulted. Beyond livid at being ridiculed and slandered, but I couldn't deny the idiocy of my situation. I'd meant it as a joke, sort of, but how could I ignore the truth blazing bright in his dark words?

"I'm twenty-four, Mr. Hawk, and you were the first man my father agreed I could spend an evening alone with. If it makes me stupid to want something I've been denied all my life, then yes, I guess I'm incredibly stupid. But you've just proven that no matter how much I wanted freedom, I love my family more, and I didn't say a proper goodbye."

The sudden need to see V and my dad overwhelmed me. Something morbid inside taunted with the horrible thought I would never see them again.

Glaring at Jethro and his imposing silence, I sucked in a breath. "This was a mistake. I'm sorry."

Gathering my train, I spun on my heels and stalked toward the huge portico and arched doorway. Blessedly my head remained clear and my feet suffered no stumbles or falls. The heaviness of my train billowed in the rush. I had no logical explanation why I suddenly needed to be around people again, but I couldn't deny the strong pull toward family.

Jethro didn't say a word. He stayed statuesque and proud in the evening darkness.

With every step I took, I expected him to call out or find some way to stop me. He didn't seem like a man who accepted no for an answer. But only silence followed, pushing me faster toward the door.

The moment I stepped through the polished entry and into the hive of heat and voices, I plucked my phone from my cleavage. There was one person in particular I wanted to speak to. A stranger I'd never heard or seen. My father had allowed me one night of freedom. I didn't want it with Jethro, but I did want it with someone else.

Maybe Kite lived close by? His number prefix said he dwelled in the United Kingdom. Like me. It wasn't a long flight to get back home.

I'd lived in London all my life, moving from the outskirts to downtown five years ago. The Weaver empire had always been based in London—right from conception. And probably always would be—if business continued to boom.

I opened a message to Kite007.

Needle&Thread: *Sorry I didn't reply before, I was busy cementing my career and ensuring I have a lifetime of servitude and sewing.*

I sighed, staring at the words. They sounded whiny and ungrateful, which I wasn't. Plus, the unsaid rule between us was no personal information. I didn't know what he did for a living or his real name or favourite food. Sex messaging was a void with no depth.

Which shows how lonely you are.

I scowled, deleting what I'd typed. I wasn't lonely. I had the best family and support in the world. I was just…tired. *Maybe I should book a holiday somewhere hot? Somewhere where I can't sew or design or get sucked back into work.* It sounded great—but one problem. I didn't want to be the loner around a pool on some tropical island. I didn't want to eat on my own by candlelight on the beach.

Take Vaughn.

I smiled. People already whispered that our relationship was too close. Going on an island getaway? That would definitely get the gossip columns buzzing.

My heart panged for the only relationship I had and how shallow it was. There was so much I wanted to say:

I want to meet you.

Please, can we skip the innuendoes and just talk?

I'm at the Nila Coal and Fire Exclusive *in the heart of Milan. I want to go for a drink with you.*

I want to get to know you.

I couldn't type any of that as it was against the rules. The unsaid rules hinted at by Kite. No personal details. No oversharing. No information of any kind but sex.

Damn rules.

Damn life.

Damn men.

My fingers flew over the screen.

Needle&Thread: *All I can think about is you and your wandering hand. I'm mad at you for coming without me, but not mad because you came while thinking of me. I've had a long night and plan on releasing my tension the moment I'm alone.*

A cynical smile twitched my lips. Kite would think I meant self-pleasuring. I really meant hitting the treadmill and running until my legs turned to jelly.

My phone came alive in my hands.

Kite007: *Me and my wandering hand missed you. By a long night I'll take it you mean on your knees servicing God in prayer. (let a man indulge in the dirty thought) Message me when you're alone. I can help with your tension.*

I looked up. Couples mingled; groups gathered. Fashion was the celebrated highlight of the evening with guests dressing in their absolute best. But it was smiles and genuine happiness that made the evening glow. I missed being happy. I hadn't laughed or smiled properly since Mum left. I could never understand how she could love us as much as she claimed, then switch off her heart…just like that.

When she'd returned from her disappearance to file for divorce from my father, she'd ruined him. Completely and utterly stole his heart and shot it to pieces on the lobby floor.

I remembered that day. I remembered thinking she'd returned with such a pretty necklace. So sparkly, it'd blinded me when she blew kisses as she walked out the door the final time.

Ever since that day, I'd been afraid of love. Afraid of the pain it could cause and how easily something so pure could turn into something so filthy.

Anger filled me. Anger I rarely let myself indulge in. I would never admit the pain my mother caused, but it was the driving force behind my workaholic nature. It was the catalyst of my life that turned me into the woman I was.

Alone. Afraid. Angry. So damn angry.

Sliding my fingers across the keypad, I sent an impulsive message.

Needle&Thread: *What if I don't want to be alone? What if I wanted help physically rather than a meaningless text? Would you help then?*

I probably shouldn't have sent it. I already knew his response. But what was so wrong with me that no man wanted to face the wrath of my father and take me for a drink?

Jethro stood up to him.

I frowned, clutching my phone. That man didn't count. He was as terrifying as my father, and his motives weren't genuine. He didn't want to listen to my tales of woe over dinner. He wasn't there to woo me. He wanted something more. And it was the more I was petrified of.

Kite007: *Okay…whose balls did you steal to write that? You know that doesn't work with me. I'm not some boy you can snap your fingers at and I'll come running.*

Pain lacerated my chest but I already expected it. Before I could reply, another message vibrated.

Kite007: *You just had to fucking do that didn't you? What do you want from me? A commitment? A relationship? You knew what this was. I thought you were having fun getting off—same as me. Why ruin what we have?*

My heart, the same useless organ that'd never been in love, cracked with agony. His anger bled from my phone, poisoning my hand. Fantastic. The only outside interaction I'd had, and it was over. But why his sudden viciousness?

Needle&Thread: *All I asked was a simple question, but you jumped down my throat. What's your deal? Don't tell me. I can guess. You're only happy when you're in charge. But guess what? I can simply delete your number and never reply to you again. You were the one who found me, remember?*

I breathed hard, huddling over my phone. I wasn't done. It was refreshing to finally allow myself to be angry. I wanted to pour it all out before I could swallow it back down again.

Needle&Thread: *I think you need to come again, Kite. Your temper is completely uncalled for and misdirected. All I implied was a meeting. One phone call. A kiss maybe if we hit it off in person. Why is that so hard for you? I'll tell you why. Because you're commitment phobic and a cheater.*

"Congratulations on your collection, Nila. I'm sure—"

I looked up into the eyes of a stranger. The woman had plump lips and wore black eyeshadow.

She paused mid-sentence. "Are you okay?"

I hated her concern. I hated that I came across as some stupid girl who could make exquisite clothing but never grace someone's arm.

I don't want to be here anymore.

I needed fresh air. I needed silence.

Him.

The silent masculinity of Jethro Hawk suddenly called to me like a cooling balm after a burning fire. He might scare me, but he had a body to touch and a mind to explore. Motives or not—he wanted me for the evening. And I was feeling reckless.

"Yes, I'm fine. Excuse me." Bunching my skirts, I dodged groups of people, heading for the exit. My phone buzzed as I reached the door.

Kite007: *Don't call me that. You lost the right to call me anything the moment you changed from tempting to annoying. I'm not a cheater or commitment phobic. And it's not hard for me to deny a meeting with you, because I already have women to fuck. I already have enough physical connections and stupid girls making demands of me. You just broke something that wasn't broken. Congratu-fucking-lations.*

My nostrils flared. *I* broke it? There was nothing to break! This whole thing had been a mistake. Unknowingly he'd taken advantage of some loser gasping for friendship. I was done being that girl.

I was done living life in black and white.

I wanted colour. I wanted passion. And there was only one man who could give me what I wanted tonight. I would use him and throw him away—just like Kite did to me.

Kite007: *If you didn't know—that was me cutting you loose. You're acting like a brat. Go and get laid. That's what I'm about to do. You want to know things about me? How about this? The woman I meant to text when I mistakenly messaged you is coming over for her long overdue reward. Don't message me again. The jerking off to your timid replies has bored me. Whoops, I just lost your number....*

My teeth gritted. My heart thundered. Pain was swamped by livid rage. How *dare* he break up with me? How dare he hurt me! How dare I let myself be hurt by a fucking arsehole who I'd never met?

I didn't care. *I don't care.*

But I did care.

I'm so stupid!

Stopping in the entrance way, my hands shook, jiggling my glowing screen. People mingled around, skirting the huge puddle of black material from my dress. I stood surrounded, yet I was all alone.

Tears pricked my eyes, but I swallowed them back. It was my own stupid fault. *I'm so stupid. Stupid...*

I sent my final message.

Needle&Thread: *When you end up alone and unloved, I hope you remember this moment. You aren't breaking up with me. I'm breaking up with* you. *Thank God I'm not a nun so I can curse the very ground you walk upon. You don't want to meet me? Fine. You just got your wish. I'm done. (hope you wank so much your dick falls off)*

Whirling around, I faced the doorway—the same doorway leading to a man who was scary and cold and silent but he was *real*. He had fingers to touch me with and a mouth to kiss. Who cared who he was? I could be stupid and use him for my own release.

Tonight I wouldn't be draining a treadmill of life. Tonight I would be riding a man who terrified me in some recess of my soul. Tonight I would be selfish and wicked and cruel.

Tonight…I would be Jethro's.

Jethro

I SAT ON my newest purchase, resting like a mechanical shadow by the curb. It didn't glint or gleam. It didn't entice or welcome. It waited in black silence ready to charge into the night.

Give her options. Don't make her suspect. Threaten only when necessary. Above all, take her without causing attention.

The rules my father told me the morning I left to fly to Milan, repeated in my head. I was obeying. Even though it was fucking hard. I struggled to balance my true nature with that of a polite gentleman, coaxing a skittish woman out for dinner.

As if I would be interested in a girl like her. Meek. Skinny. Beyond fucking sheltered it was insane.

Grabbing the throttle of my bike, I waged with ignoring my father's rules and stalking into the venue and stealing Nila Weaver in front of everyone. She could scream, shout—it wouldn't make a difference. But that wasn't *allowed*.

The other option was I could just fuck off and kidnap her from her hotel room.

She has to come willingly.

My father's voice again. Kidnapping was the last resort.

I growled under my breath.

I'd let her go, not because of some decency, or concern of what would happen to her family's happiness, or even the upcoming pain in her future. No, I let her go, because I was my father's son and followed a plan.

I was a hunter. Skilled with both bow and arrow and gun.

The chase was the best part. And knowing I had the power to snuff out Nila Weaver's life the moment I caught her gave me a certain…thrill.

That was the only reason I restrained myself and followed the rules.

I had no secrets of why I would stain my hands with her blood. I had no misplaced vendettas or agendas. Everything that would come to pass was for one simple and undisputable fact.

There was a debt to be paid. And I was the method of extraction. Plain and simple.

I'm a Hawk. She's a Weaver.

That was all I needed to know.

In the library a week ago, while sipping on a ten thousand pound bottle of cognac, my father proceeded to tell me a little of our history. He told me gruesome things. Dastardly things. Tears shed. Blood spilled. He told me what happened to Nila's mother.

He also told me why every firstborn Weaver girl had a stain upon her life. I understood it. I accepted it. I was given the task to uphold my family's honour. And I fully intended to extract payment as meticulously and as painfully as possible.

Because it was my task.

It wasn't often I was given the opportunity to make my bastard of a father proud. I didn't intend to let him down.

Even though I wouldn't enjoy it.

Nila Weaver would be my greatest trophy.

Oh, yes. I would enjoy ruining her. I liked playing with the inner mechanics of people. I liked to break them smoothly, gently, ruthlessly. I liked to think I transformed creatures from their present to their potential.

Pity once Nila was transformed she wouldn't be allowed to enjoy her evolution. She would be dead. That was the final toll. That was her future.

To kill something so naïvely pretty…

It made me angry to think of such delicate perfection snuffed out. But there was no point thinking of the end when the chase had just begun.

"Nice bike."

My head snapped up, eyes locking onto my prey. The same prey who'd run yet returned.

She'd returned? *I was right before. She truly is stupid.*

Nila drifted forward, threading and unthreading her fingers. I didn't move or utter a sound. She responded to my silence—like everything. I'd learned that cursing and yelling could be frightening—but silence…it was the empty void where enemies' fears polluted. Stay quiet long enough and horror would be struck with one whisper instead of a multitude of profanities.

She waved at my bike, her eyes wider than before…darker than before.

Deciding to grant her a reply, I said, "It's my version of accessorising." The sleek Harley-Davidson was a new purchase.

Stroking the throttle, I tilted my head. Her dusky skin had colour. Her pronounced cheekbones were flushed, trailing residual temper down her neck. Something had happened. Something had upset her.

Did she find her father, only for him to disown her and send her back to me?

I frowned. Could Archibald Weaver truly send his only daughter not once, but twice, to her death? He knew what awaited her. He knew what would happen if he didn't give her up. But was family honour that strong? Or was there more to this debt than I'd been told?

Either way, it was time to go. Time to begin her nightmare.

"You returned."

She nodded. "I returned. I want something from you. And I'm not going to be shy about asking."

A flicker of surprise caught me unaware. She came across shy and timid, but there lurked steel in her voice. Little did she know what I wanted from her in return.

"Fair enough. I have something to discuss with you."

Don't make her suspect.

"What?"

Your future. Your death.

"Nothing important, but we need to go."

Time to begin. The time is nigh to pay your debts.

Nila came closer, shedding the tameness, and embracing courage. I would've been intrigued if I didn't already know everything about her.

Such a silly girl. A silly toy.

Whatever she wanted from me, I'd oblige. After all, she'd been given to me to do as I pleased.

And everyone knows you don't give a pet to a killer.

Nila

"GET ON."

I blinked. "Excuse me?"

Jethro didn't move. He didn't look condescending or annoyed or anything other than cold and collected. Nothing seemed to interest him. I thought I could use him for sex? He didn't look like he knew what a smile was, let alone passion.

His legs bunched beneath the dark charcoal of his trousers, steadying the heavy motorcycle between them. "I said, get on. We're leaving."

I laughed. What a ludicrous suggestion. Waving down my front, I hoped he wasn't blind, because no one could ignore the kilograms worth of black diamantes or acres of material I wore. "I struggled to get here in a limousine. There's no way I can perch on the back of a stupid motorcycle."

Jethro's lips quirked. "Come closer. I'll fix that."

My heart jumped; I clutched my phone tighter. No response from Kite. *Which is a* good *thing.* I just had to keep telling myself that. I never wanted to hear from him again. "Fix it how?"

"Come here and I'll show you." His eyes drifted down the front of my dress.

I'd been around powerful, attractive men all my life. Both my father and brother were well known for being eligible bachelors, but they lacked something that Jethro held in abundance.

Mystery.

Everything about him spoke of trickery and wile. He'd barely spoken, yet I *felt* his requests. For some stupid reason, it felt as if he'd trained me with his silence to be alert, ready, eager to please.

I hated his effortless power.

Backing away, I shook my head. "I won't."

A small smile graced his lips, golden eyes flashing. "That wasn't very polite. I gave you a request, kindly delivered, respectfully even." His fingers tightened around the handle bars. "Should I ask again, or will you rethink your reply?"

A trickle of fear blustered down my neck. I knew that glint in his eye. Vaughn would get it when we were younger. It meant destruction. It meant getting their own way. It meant a world of pain if I didn't obey. And for some reason, I didn't think a wedgie and being tickled until I couldn't breathe counted as pain in Jethro's dimension.

Clutching the bodice that'd taken me weeks to hand-sew, I took another step backward. "I'm not being impolite; I'm stating the obvious. If you wish to leave, we need a different method of transportation." Speaking so formally sounded odd after screaming via text message to Kite. "And besides, I don't want to leave yet. I promised myself I'd ask you something, and I'm not going anywhere until I do."

God, Nila. What are you doing?

Nerves attacked my stomach, but I kept my stance. I wouldn't back down. Not this time.

Jethro shook his head, displacing his longish salt-and-pepper hair. His smooth face remained expressionless with patience, but it didn't relieve—it terrified. With precision born of wealth and confidence, he kicked the stand down and placed the bike into a resting position. Swinging his leg over the machine, he climbed the curb and hunted.

No. Don't let him touch you.

I stumbled backward, a slight edge of dizziness catching me off guard.

Jethro caught me, placing his large, cold hands on my waist.

I froze, breathing shallowly. Shoving away the moment of wobbliness, I fixated on his strong jaw and glinting diamond pin.

The temperature of his touch seeped through the ruffles on my hips, bringing with it fear manifesting like icicles over an innocent dawn.

"What's wrong with you?" Jethro jerked me closer, peering into my eyes. The first sign of animation lurked in their golden depths. It wasn't concern though, merely annoyance. "Are you ill?" Annoyance turned to carefully hidden anger.

I swallowed hard, hating my condition all over again. To him, I would come across as weak. He wouldn't understand the strength it took to live a normal life while shackled to an improperly balanced form. If anything, it made me stronger.

"No, I'm not ill. Not that you're worried for my health." Twitching in his hold, I searched for a way free. But his touch only tightened. Blowing a blue-black strand from my eye, I added, "It's not contagious. I suffer from vertigo. That's all. Google it."

That's all. I scrape my knees if I get out of bed too fast and faint if I swivel my head too quick, but that's all.

Jethro scowled. "Perhaps you shouldn't wear such heavy clothing." He plucked the dense material and delicate stitching on my waist. "It's a hindrance and delaying my night's activities."

My eyes flared. Night's activities?

Perhaps he had the same conclusion of where we'd end up? Captive in his strong hands, I stared up. I wasn't short for a woman, but Jethro had at least half a foot on me. He didn't move, only watched as if I were an interesting specimen he couldn't decide to enjoy or throw away.

My breathing grew shallow the longer he held me.

Dropping my gaze to his lips, it didn't help my anxiety at having them so close. *It's now or never.*

I knew nothing about him. He scared me. But he was a man. I was a woman. And once, just once, I wanted pleasure.

"I want something from you," I murmured.

He stilled. "What exactly makes you think you're in a position to ask something of me?"

I shook my head. "I'm not asking."

A moment thickened between us. His nostrils twitched. "Go on…"

"Take me for a drink. I want to get to know you."

Not quite what I wanted to ask, but I couldn't be so bold.

He laughed once. "Believe me, Ms. Weaver, I'll save you from a mundane conversation. The most you'll ever know about me is my name. Everything else…let's just say, ignorance is bliss."

His aftershave of woods and leather came over me again. The chilliness in his gaze warned not to push, but I couldn't help myself. Not after the way Kite treated me.

"Bliss…that's a word I don't understand."

Jethro cocked his head, the trace of annoyance coming again. "What exactly are you trying to do?"

A rush of wobbliness hit me. I looked over my shoulder at the café across the street. "Have a nightcap with me. Over there." I motioned with my head. I didn't care in the least I wore a huge gown or that the coffee shop was empty. The couch in the window looked comfy, and I wasn't ready to have this small freedom destroyed.

He looked to the small venue, a flicker of confusion filling his eyes. "You—" Cutting himself off, he straightened and let me go. "Fine. If that's all you want, I see no reason why I can't prolong our true agenda for thirty minutes." Capturing my elbow, he half-dragged, half-marched me across the street.

My heart sank at the lack of romance and anticipation. I'd hoped he'd relax a little—knowing I was interested—and drop the chilly façade.

What if it's not a façade? His demeanour was steadfast and engrained. I doubted he'd ever been carefree or impulsive.

The propulsion was fast, too fast for someone like me with the balance of a damn butterfly, but his hold was firm and granted a certain safety.

Striding over the curb, Jethro yanked open the glass door, scowling at the bell jingling above. A young Italian girl looked up, smiling in welcome.

The rich aroma of coffee and warmth instantly stole the stress from my blood from Kite, the show, and Jethro's company.

"Sit." Jethro let me go, pointing toward the faded yellow settee with purple and orange throw cushions. "And don't move."

I stood frozen. Jethro had no wish to be here, especially with me. What the hell was going on? First my father pushed me on him, then Jethro barely tolerated my company. *Am I that repulsive?*

"Wait," I said. "Aren't you going to ask what I want?"

Jethro raised an eyebrow. "No. Want to know why?"

I did. But I didn't want to play his ridiculous game. The night had turned from promising to disastrous.

When I didn't reply, Jethro waved his hand. "It doesn't matter what you prefer in beverages. You only get one request and you got it. I'm here against my plans; therefore, you'll drink what I give you."

My mouth parted, amazement stealing my ability to shout the incomprehensible phrases jumbled inside. *Seriously?* Who was this man?

Jethro strode away, leaving me gawking at his powerful back dressed in an immaculate, tailored suit. He completely ignored me while he ordered.

Not wanting to stand like a dismissed damsel, I moved to the couch and sat in a cloud of midnight-galaxy material. The underwire and other tricks to keep my dress buoyant argued against sitting, but my feet breathed a sigh of gratefulness.

Jethro returned with two cups of coffee. Espresso. Tiny cups, no biscotti, or anything to prolong something he obviously didn't want to do. Placing the hot drink in front of me on the low table, he sipped his own, glaring at me over the rim.

I broke eye contact, collecting the cup of black liquid. Truth be told, I hated coffee. I'd only suggested the café to delay whatever he'd planned that was so urgent.

Inhaling the strong caffeine, I pretended to sip while sneaking glimpses at the mystery beside me. Did it matter he was an arrogant arse who didn't know the difference between cruel and polite? He had a killer body, distinguished good looks, and a presence that screamed domination in the bedroom. I could choose worse for a night of guilt-free sex.

Sitting taller, I said, "So…the thing I wanted to ask you…"

What are you doing? He's not a nice person. And he's got the patience of a Doberman.

Jethro clenched his jaw, swirling his coffee. "I won't answer, do, or respond to any more requests. Drink your coffee. We're running late."

I ignored that and tried to break the ice between us. "You seem to know my father. What obligations—"

"No questions." Jethro tossed his head back, swallowing the double shot in one go. Licking his lips, he carefully placed his cup on the table, eyeing my untouched one.

The unease of why my father had permitted me to go out with such an insensitive bastard came back. I feared there was a lot I wasn't aware of.

Running a hand through his greying hair, Jethro suddenly shoved my overflowing skirts off the couch and slid closer. So close his body heat seared my naked arms, prickling me with intensity.

I gulped, curling my hands in my lap.

Jethro bristled. "Whatever you think you're doing, it won't work. I will neither make small talk nor enter into meaningful conversation. You request to visit a coffee shop, yet don't touch what I bought you." He sighed, tension tightening his eyes. "I'm done playing silly games. Tell me what I need to do to make you come without making a fuss, and I'll do it."

My heart stopped. Anxiety roared back into existence. Why had I thought I could seduce this man? I had no hope, especially when he was obviously pissed off rather than intrigued. Linking my fingers together, I said quietly, "Why would I make a fuss? Where exactly do you want to take me?"

Please say a hotel and admit your attitude is all an act. Please say my brother hired you to play the horrible arsehole only to sweep me off my feet in a night of escorted bliss.

I should've known better than to wish for such things.

Jethro frowned. "What did I just say? No questions." Grabbing my wrist, he tugged me closer, crushing my dress between us. "I don't have time for games. Tell me what you want." His mouth was so close, his brooding temper filling a bubble around us.

My eyes dropped to his lips. All I could picture was one kiss. One beautifully gentle, romantic kiss that turned my insides molten and my mind to stars.

I breathed shallowly, unable to raise my gaze to his.

He half-smiled. "*That's* what you want?"

I blinked, dispelling the haze of intoxication he'd placed me under. "I didn't say anything."

Letting my wrist go, he trailed his fingertips up my arm. I shivered, loving and hating his masterful touch. "You didn't have to. I should've known this would happen."

My eyes flared. "Known?" Embarrassment came swift and hot. Was I so obvious? So needy?

"No questions," he snapped. Sighing heavily, he added, "You forget your life is rather public, Ms. Weaver. And I happen to know you're not…experienced." Cupping my chin, he ran the pad of his thumb over my bottom lip.

I froze.

Jethro's face didn't soften or beguile, but his voice

dropped to a murmur. His masculine scent threaded around me transporting me from the coffee shop and into his control.

"What is it you want? A kiss? A caress?" His voice echoed like a deep baritone until I felt his question in my bones.

Leaning closer, his mouth hovered over mine. He smelled decadently of coffee. "Do you *ache* for something? Do you lie in bed at night and crave a man's touch?" His breath feathered over my lips, drugging me. "How wet do you get? Answer my questions, Ms. Weaver. Tell me how you pleasure yourself while fantasising about a man fucking you."

I couldn't feel any part of my body apart from the firm hold he had on my chin and the tingling of my lips. I couldn't think apart from the dark visions he coaxed in my head of nakedness and fingers and stolen caresses.

"Tell me. Convince me," Jethro tormented, bringing his mouth closer. Only a feather breadth away—a phantom kiss, but it made every inch throb.

"Yes," I whispered. "Yes, I fantasise. Yes, I ache." Wishing I could pull away and hide my vulnerability, I added, "That's what I wanted. From you."

Everything you painted and more.

"When you imagine a nameless male taking you, do you picture champagne, massages, and soul-shattering sex?" His nose nudged mine.

I nodded, eyelids drooping, begging him to kiss me.

His head tilted, grazing the corner of my mouth with his. A tease. A half-kiss. A promise. His mouth trailed to my ear. "You naïve little girl. If I took you, you wouldn't be adored or worshipped. You'd be used and *fucked*. I have no patience for sweet."

I opened my eyes, fighting against the thick lust in my blood.

Jethro sneered. "Pity you didn't say you fantasised about a man using you, abusing you. Pity you didn't admit to darker desires such as bondage and pain. Then perhaps I might've granted your wish." He trailed his lips over my cheekbone. His touch was condescending rather than erotic. "Now tell me, Ms. Weaver. Knowing my certain appetites, are you still wet for me? Is that what you're asking for? My tongue. My attention? My…" He nuzzled away my hair, biting painfully on the shell of my ear. "…cock."

I wanted to deny the flutter in my heart and the intense heat billowing in my core. I wanted to be outraged at his crudeness and blatant sexual thrill. But I couldn't. Because despite never entertaining the idea of violence with sex, I couldn't stop the undeniable allure.

Pulling back, Jethro whispered, "Don't turn timid on me. Say it. Say what you want."

I was no longer human; I was liquid. Hot, pliable liquid just waiting for some force to reshape me. Everything he'd said flared a need inside until a fever broke across my brow.

Dropping my eyes, I whispered, "I want…I want…"

Jethro tightened his fingers on my jaw. "Say it." His eyes flashed and the misconception that he didn't know passion dissolved. He knew it. He wielded it. He hid it beneath layers and layers of mystery I would never hope to unravel.

Taking a shaky breath, cursing the damn corset, I said, "I want your mouth."

He nodded. "Fine. But I'll have yours first." His thumb stroked my lips again, breaking the seal of my red lipstick, and penetrating my mouth.

I froze, eyes wide and locked on his. "Where do you want it?" His voice dropped to a barely murmured curse—impossible to ignore, deadly to my ears and body.

He didn't care about the waitress or that anyone on the darkened street could see us. He just pinned me with unswerving golden eyes and hooked his thumb against my tongue.

I couldn't speak. His large palm held me immobile while his finger rendered me silent. I didn't know what to do. Should I suck? Bite? Do nothing?

Jethro smiled, it wasn't his usual icy edge, but it wasn't soft either. "Follow your instincts. You want to suck, so suck." He forced his thumb deeper into my mouth, eyes darkening.

He so easily placed me into a position of submission, but I'd never felt so powerful. Closing my lips, I sucked. Once.

His jaw clenched, but nothing more.

I did it again, licking his finger with an eager tongue. My mouth filled with liquid, tasting him. Wanting him. Every suck sent a wave of insatiable need to my core, making me wet.

Jethro's shoulders tensed. "See? You didn't need to tell me what you wanted. Your body does that for you. You've surprised me, and that isn't an easy thing to do." My dress rustled as he wrapped an arm around my waist, dragging me against his hard body.

I went willingly, trapped in so many ways. My mind was consumed with only him. There was peace in that moment. Lust yes, feverishness definitely, but also serenity at the complete attention he demanded. I didn't have to think of my family, my company, my endless work schedule.

I was nothing but flesh and blood and bone.

I was need personified, and only Jethro could put out the fire he'd cajoled.

His lips brushed against my ear again. I tensed for the bite of teeth. "Know what else your body tells me?"

I shook my head, swirling my tongue around his thumb. My core clenched; my mind blanked.

"You need something. You want something that you're not ready to understand." Jethro placed a delicate kiss against my jaw. "You need it so bad you'd allow me to run my hand up your knee, between your legs, and sink my fingers deep inside you this very second. You'd open your innocent thighs, even with witnesses, and moan as I sank my cock deeper than anyone."

A bubble formed in my chest, twisting and glistening with a mixture of denial and agreement.

His thumb pressed hard, pinning my tongue below.

I jerked, eyes tearing wide.

"You'd let me drag you into some sleazy alley, tear off your dress, and…"

I didn't want to hear the rest. But I did. Oh, how I did. He'd taken the power of speech away. I couldn't deny anything he said. And I didn't want to. For the first time in my life, I had something real. Cheap and shallow, just like Kite, but hot-blooded and absolute.

I would willingly trade my flawless reputation for one night of sordid incredibleness. *What does that make me?*

I flinched, answering my own question. *Lonely*. I hated that word more than any other in the dictionary.

Jethro's thumb slinked slowly from my mouth, holding me firm. "You'd let me make you scream, Ms. Weaver, and because of that willingness, I would never bow to what you want."

The heat generated from the intense conversation dispersed, faster and faster. He curled his lips. "Whatever would your father say if he knew his daughter secretly wanted to be *fucked* against an alley wall by a stranger?"

The crudeness of his words slammed me back to reality.

He dropped his hand, and plucked a napkin from the table. Imprisoning my gaze, he slowly wiped his glistening thumb, before tossing the tissue into his empty coffee cup. "I dare you to deny any of that. Or pretend you didn't want every inch of me." He smirked at the double entendre.

The flush of mortification crested over my breasts to my cheeks. My tongue bruised from his rough handling, my mouth empty from tasting him. I couldn't sit there and be ridiculed any longer.

This was karma, and it stung like hell.

Grabbing the mountains of fabric wedged around me, I tried to stand—unsuccessfully. "I'm leaving. I can't—"

"If you can't speak the truth, I don't want to hear your other excuses or reasons on why you suddenly need to run. You're not permitted to leave my side, so be a good girl and fucking listen and obey." His voice whipped me, but his body remained immaculate and collected. The two dynamics of temper and poise pierced my stupid haze, slamming me back into fear.

Who *was* this man?

And why didn't I run the moment I set eyes upon him? Something wasn't right. Something was building, rushing toward a conclusion I wanted no part in.

Jethro stood upright, jerking me to my feet. "I take by your silence you've made a sensible decision and acquiesced. I'm also assuming that this—whatever this was—is over?" His fingers bit into my bicep, shaking me. "Stop acting the fool and realize what is happening."

Anger replaced my embarrassment. It was like Kite all over again, only worse, because this was real and I had nowhere to hide. "I have no idea what's happening, and I'm not going anywhere with you. You've proved that you find me gullible, stupid, and unworthy of your precious time, so leave. I'm not keeping you here." Twisting my elbow, I tried to get free. "I don't want to do this anymore."

Jethro smiled coldly. "Ah, there's the conundrum, Ms. Weaver. You're not keeping me. But *I'm* keeping *you*."

I stopped with my hand over his, unsuccessfully trying to pry his fingers off my arm. "What?" The dreaded drunkenness of vertigo took that moment to tilt my world.

Jethro took my weakness as an opportunity, pulling me toward the door. He didn't give me any support other than the harsh hold on my upper arm, leaving my untouched coffee on the table. "I'm leaving. And you're coming with me."

The door jangled as we exited in a flurry of bustle and feathers. I gasped as a frosty gust cut through the warmth lingering on my skin, decimating all remainders of the café.

Slamming my heels into the pavement, I snarled, "You seem to have the wrong information. I'm not going anywhere with you."

Jethro didn't reply, dragging me effortlessly across the road to the shadowy entrance of an alley and his bike.

An alley?

He couldn't mean what he'd threatened…could he?

You want me to make you scream.

I fought harder. But no matter how much I struggled, he didn't break his stride or look back.

Tripping forward, I winced as my flesh bruised beneath his hold. I angled my nails, preparing to drag them over his forearm, but he stepped onto the curb and yanked me forward. The inertia propelled me into a spin, slamming me painfully against his motorcycle.

My black hair whirled over my shoulder, sticking to the fear perspiring on my chest. I struggled to keep up—to believe how stupid I'd been. I prided myself on being smart, but I'd allowed the temptation of sex to cloud my judgement.

Jethro glowered; his suit as crisp as his unflappable control. "My information is perfectly correct. And you *are* going somewhere with me. Climb on."

I tore my elbow from his hold and shoved his chest. "Wrong. Let me go."

He growled under his breath. "Stop, before you get hurt."

I pushed him again, focusing on the ridiculousness of my night, rather than the rapidly expanding terror in my heart. "I told you. I came in a limo; there is no way I can travel on a two-wheeled death machine."

Jethro rolled his shoulders, maintaining his cool. "I gave you one rule—never ask questions. I'm giving you another—don't ever argue with me."

My heart raced. Glancing around, I searched for late night stragglers, party goers, moon-light walkers—anyone who could intervene and save me. The roads were empty. No one. Not even a scurrying rodent.

"Please, I don't know what game you're playing—"

He shook his head, exasperation in his eyes. "Game? This isn't a fucking game." Glaring at my dress, he encroached on my space. Pressing his lips together briefly, he muttered, "I hope you're wearing something beneath this."

My lungs stuck together. "What? Why?"

"Because you're going to be indecent if you're not." With a savage jerk, he tore the endless seams, stitching, and hard work of my dress. The rip sounded like a scream to my ears. Horror swarmed as the outer layer fluttered to the ground, followed by organza, feathers, and beadwork.

My jaw hung open. "No—"

Jethro spun me around, his hands skating over my lower back. "You're like a damn pass the parcel." With strong fingers, he tore the second layer of heavy ebony silk.

The sound of shredding broke my heart. All that work! My father would be pissed to see his expensive material littering the dirty pavement. My blood existed in the needlepoint from pricking my fingers. My tears soaked the train from overworking. He couldn't do this!

I couldn't speak—struck mute by shock.

"Good God, another?" Jethro spun me back to face him. I swished in the remaining starchy petticoats—the tool beneath the dress that granted such volume.

I can't do this anymore.

I plastered my hands down my front, seizing the remainder of my gown. "No, pleas—"

Jethro ignored me. With one last brutal tug, he tore the petticoat off, disposing it on top of the already ruined layers.

Tears glassed my eyes. "Oh, my God. What did you do?" The cool Milan air swirled around my naked legs, disappearing up the thigh-length satin skirt I wore to prevent chafing from the petticoat underwire. My entire ensemble—destroyed. I'd been the only female in a household of men. I'd spent an entire lifetime covering up my girlish body with lace and camisoles and tulle. Femininity was something I created rather than lived. To see it demolished on a filthy sidewalk enraged me to the point of tyranny.

Gone were my tears. I embraced furiousness. "How *could* you?!"

Shoving him away, I fell to my knees, trying to gather the

rhinestones and swatches of handmade lace. "You—you ruined it!" All around scattered couture fashion. Diamantes glittered on bland concrete. Feathers twitched, dancing away on the breeze.

"I'll ruin a lot more before I'm through." Jethro's barely uttered words existed, then…didn't, snatched by a gust of wind.

I glared up at the man I'd stupidly returned for—all because a stranger hurt my feelings. A man I'd allowed to manipulate me and make me heinously wet in a coffee shop. "Does it make you feel better? Destroying other's things? Don't you care that you just ruined something that took hours upon hours to create? What sort of cruel—"

"Stop." He held up a finger, scolding me like a little child. "Rule number three. I don't like raised voices. So shut up and stand."

We glared; silence was a heavy entity between us.

He was right. I was so, so stupid. He'd successfully hurt me more than anyone since my mother left. His callousness gave no room for hope or tears. And I knew it all along. I'd seen his coldness. I'd felt his hardened will. Yet it didn't stop me from being an utter fool.

Grabbing a puddle of cloth, I yelled, "Leave me alone!"

"Goddammit, you're testing me." He ducked suddenly, grabbing my bicep and hauling me to my feet. He shook me—hard. My corset dug into my hipbones now that it had no bustle or layers to rest upon.

"You don't get to ask any more questions. You don't get to yell or act ridiculous. This is happening. This is your future. Nothing you say or do will change that—it will only change the level of pain you receive." He shoved me backward against his bike. "Your dress is conveniently no longer an issue. Get on. We're leaving."

Fury exploded through my heart, thankfully keeping my terror at bay.

Don't think about his threat. Focus on making him yell.

Loudness. I needed commotion to garner attention and safety.

"You just ruined my showpiece. That dress was already sold to a high-end boutique in Berlin! You think I want to go anywhere with you after you ruined over two months' worth of work? You're insane. I'll tell you how this is going to go—"

"Ms. Weaver, shut the fuck up. I'm done with this charade." His face remained impassive, but the muscles beneath his suit bristled. Moving horribly fast, he tugged my long, unfettered hair, crowding me against his bike. Wincing against the pain in my scalp, I tripped, splaying over the leather seat.

Looking around quickly, he relaxed when he noticed we were still alone. "If you knew me, you'd know how I react to incorrect statements about my mental health. If you were smart, you would know never to raise your voice and to maintain proper conduct in public."

He bowed his head, brushing his nose threateningly against my ear. "But seeing as you *don't* know me, I'll withhold the punishment—for now. But a word of warning, Ms. Weaver. Just because I don't lower myself to the unattractive use of volume, doesn't mean I'm not pissed. I'm very fucking pissed. I gave you an order, and you've disobeyed numerous times already. This is the last time I'll ask politely."

Pulling away, he grabbed my middle and with strength that terrified, plucked me from the ground and plonked me on the back of his bike, side-saddle.

Giving a mock salute, Jethro said, "Thank you for obliging me. I'm so glad you decided to climb aboard." With a scowl, he noticed my high heels. Dropping to one knee, he tore them off my feet, throwing them over his shoulder. They disappeared in the clouds of decimated fabric behind him.

I truly was Cinderella, only my prince threw away the glass slipper and stole me away before midnight struck. My prince was evil. My prince was the villain.

I couldn't breathe.

Run. Kick him. Do not let him take you.

All manner of horrible situations ran wild in my head. I'd been brought up in a safe neighbourhood, instilled with common-sense and morals. Yet nothing had prepared me to fight for my life against a lunatic who came across as sane.

"You can't do this. I don't want to go with you." I tried to jump off, but Jethro's sleek bulk prevented me from moving. He loomed upright like a terrible sentence—a judgement of my past and present. "You have no choice. You're coming with me. Your wishes have no relevance."

Stabbing him in the chest with my fingertip, I shouted, "My wishes are completely relevant. You can't take me against my will. That's called kidnapping." My body flushed with hot anger. "Let. Me. Go. Before I scream."

Vaughn. Shit, I wanted my brother. The amount of times he protected me growing up from bees, and badgers, and boys who picked on me at school.

Vaughn!

Jethro shook his head. "It's too late. For any of that. And don't scream. I don't do well with screamers." He chuckled mirthlessly. "Unless I'm the reason for said scream and we're in private."

I ignored the 'scream topic' and focused on the horrible ultimatum. Too late? *What's too late?* I wasn't on some countdown where my life ended as I knew it. I didn't agree to any of this!

I didn't, but maybe father did.

The thought stopped me like a knitting needle to the heart. He'd introduced me to Jethro—over any other man. He'd encouraged me to go with him—against my brother's wishes.

Jethro might've been able to hoodwink my father, but I saw his true colours, and I wasn't going to tolerate it any longer. This fiasco had gone on long enough.

I opened my mouth to scream. My lungs expanded with a plea. "Help—"

Jethro lashed out, slapping a cool palm over my lips. The first sign of uncontrollable emotion blazed in his eyes. He sighed heavily, shaking his head. "I'd hoped you'd be more intelligent than that."

I slapped him.

The sharp ringing of flesh against flesh froze time. I didn't move or breathe or blink. Neither did Jethro.

We stared at each other until all I knew was gold from his eyes. The air dropped from autumn to blustery winter the longer we glowered, freezing over with his temper. It could've been a second or ten, but it was Jethro who broke the brittleness between us.

His cold fingers trailed from my mouth to my throat. Wrapping tight. Unforgiving. The action showed the truth—the inhuman truth. This man was fastidiously groomed and softly spoken, but beneath it all raged a devil in disguise. His touch told endless information of the man he tried to hide. He was the ultimate in camouflage.

He was iron-fisted and remorseless.

Tilting my neck with bruising fingers, he murmured, "Obey and I won't hurt you. Fight me and I'll make you scream."

Every muscle in my body jolted. The decimation of my dress no longer mattered. All I cared about was running as far and as fast as I could. Tears bubbled in my chest; I bit my lip to stop the rapidly building sob from escaping.

Jethro never let go of my throat. "I'm not here to kidnap you. I'm not here to knock you out or drug you. Call me old-fashioned, but I'd hoped you'd come willingly and prevent both of us an inconvenience." Stroking my hair with his free hand, he cupped the back of my skull. "You're probably wondering why I said you have no choice but to come with me. Because I'm a fair man and believe in equality—even between hunter and prey—I'll tell you."

His breath was the only warm thing about him, scalding my skin with words I didn't want to hear. "I'm here to extract a debt. The reason for that debt will be revealed when I'm good and ready. The method of payment for that debt is entirely up to you."

My brain swam, trying to understand. "What—"

His fingers tightened, cutting off my air supply. Choking, the instinct to fight overrode my frozen terror. I squirmed, scratching my nails over his wrists.

My nails didn't affect him—if anything, it made him calmer. Tutting under his breath, he said, "The first thing you should know about me is I *never* forget. If you draw blood trying to get free, I'll only repay in kind. It's worth remembering, Ms. Weaver."

His gaze fell to my clawing fingers, tightening his own until I fought against what I truly wanted and let them slide from his wrists.

"Good girl," he murmured. Pulling back, he unwound his digits one at a time from my throat. Meticulous in slowness. Terrifying in control.

I only repay in kind. His voice echoed in my head. I balled my hands in my lap, hoping I wouldn't lash out or do anything he might deem repayable. I wanted to hurt him so much I trembled. I wanted him bleeding on the pavement so I could *run*.

Standing tall, Jethro glared, waiting to see what I would do.

I was half his size—and without witnesses, I was helpless. I'd never taken self-defence or thought I'd be in a situation that required it. The treadmill trimmed my figure, but didn't give me muscle to fight.

What could I do but obey? I didn't move. I couldn't. Even my vertigo didn't dare make me queasy when I was trapped in his savage golden eyes.

A moment ticked past before he nodded curtly. "I'm glad you're acting with more decorum. To ensure that behaviour, I'll share one piece of information about the debt with you." He ran a finger along his bottom lip. "You are the only one who can repay. You must come of your own free will. You are the sacrifice."

I swallowed, flinching at the bruising around my larynx.

His level voice lulled me into thinking I had a chance at escape. *Keep him talking. Get him to care.* "Sacrifice?" I instantly hated the word.

His eyes narrowed. "A sacrifice is something you do or give up for the greater good. All of this could stop...you have the power."

It could? The promise of freedom hung in the night-sky, taunting me.

I shifted on the seat, shivering from the cold. "If I have the power, why do I feel as if you're laughing behind my back?" Steeling myself, I snapped, "Whatever you might think of me, I can read between the lines of what you're not saying. What are the consequences if I don't go with you?"

I felt ridiculous talking of debts and consequences. None of this made sense, but a horrible sensation slithered up my back. A memory that I'd buried...from a long time ago.

"You have no choice, Arch. I can't explain it, but you, me, no one can stop this. My only regret is meeting you."

My father huffed, whirling around in the drawing room of our eight bedroom manor. "Your only regret? What about V and Nila? What should I tell them? What should I say when they ask why their mother abandoned them?"

My mother, with her glossy ebony hair and dusky skin, stood tall and fearless, but from my hidden spot by the stairs I knew the truth. She wasn't fearless—far from it. She was petrified. "You tell them I loved them but I should never have given them life. Especially Nila. Hide her, Arch. Don't let them know. Change your name. Run. Don't let the debt get her, too."

The memory had ended abruptly thanks to Vaughn throwing a soccer ball at my head and shattering the final moments my parents had together. That had been the last time I ever saw her.

I rubbed my palm against my chest, cursing the tightness around my heart. Confusion weighed heavily, equally as pressing as despair.

Jethro smiled. "I'm glad you're being more reasonable.

That is one question I will answer. The consequences of not coming with me are Vaughn and Archibald Weaver, amongst other things."

My whole world flipped upside down—and this time it wasn't vertigo.

"Your life for theirs." He shrugged. "Simple really. But don't worry about the details. There's the fine print and endless history lessons to explain."

My heart stopped. My life for theirs? *He has to be joking.* I didn't know if I should be screaming in terror or laughing with amazement. This couldn't be real. It had to be a farce.

"You can't be serious. You expect me to believe you?"

Jethro lost his ice, sliding straight into arctic winter. "You think I *care* if you don't believe me? Do you think all of this is bullshit and you can somehow argue with me?"

My heart jack-knifed. He was so sure. So resolute. No hint of worry that his scam might be revealed.

It isn't a joke.

Jethro lowered his voice. "I'll let you in on another secret about me. I never do things by half. I never take chances. And I never hunt alone." Leaning closer, he finished, "Ever since I set eyes on you, your family has been watched. They're being judged. And if you so much as sneeze wrong, that judgement will turn into something a lot more invasive. Do you understand?"

I couldn't reply. All I could picture was Vaughn and my father being exterminated like vermin.

"Say another word and I'll end them, Ms. Weaver." With a glacial glare, Jethro grabbed the handle bars and swung his leg over the black powder-coated machine. Every inch was black. No chrome or colour anywhere.

Shit, what do I do? I had to run. *Run!*

But I couldn't. Not now he'd threatened my family. Not now my brain had unlocked a memory adding weight to Jethro's lunatic suggestions. Not now I *believed.*

A debt.

I didn't know what it was. It could've been code for something I didn't understand or literal and requiring payback. But one thing I knew, I couldn't risk not obeying.

I loved my family. I adored my brother. I wouldn't chance their lives.

I jumped as the ignition growled to life, tearing through the silence, and somehow granting me strength in its ferocity. Kicking the stand away, Jethro took the weight of the bike.

He didn't wear a helmet or offer me one. I expected him to turn around and deliver more information or demands, but all he did was reach behind, steal my arm, and place it around his hips. The moment my hand rested on him, he let me go, unknowingly giving me a safe harbour but with an anchor I already despised.

I looked longingly at the building where my brother and father mingled with fashionistas and the only world I knew. I silently begged them to come running out and laugh at my stunned, fear-filled face yelling 'we fooled you.'

But nothing. The doors remained closed. Answers hidden. Future unknown.

I'm alone.

I'm being stolen for a debt only I can repay. A debt I know nothing about.

I was idiotic to wish for more than what I had.

Now, I had nothing.

With a twist of his wrist, Jethro fed gas to his mechanical beast and we shot forward into darkness.

The Milan airport welcomed me back.

It felt like an eternity since I flew in, though in reality it'd only been two days. My skin was icy, and despite my repellent dislike for Jethro, I hadn't been able to stop huddling against him while he broke speed limits and took corners at hyper-speed on his death machine. My tiny skirt and sleeveless corset weren't meant for gallivanting around Milan so late.

Pulling into a short term parking bay, he killed the engine and kicked down the stand. I immediately sat back, unwinding my arms from around his waist.

The fear remained in my heart, growing thicker with every beat. I couldn't look at the so-called gentleman without swallowing a cocktail of murderous rage and teary terror.

His profile showed a man with a five o' clock shadow, windswept thick hair, and an edge that catapulted him from sexy to dangerous. He stood out from a crowd. He drew need and desire effortlessly. But there was nothing tame or kind or normal. He reeked of manipulation and control.

He's an iceberg.

The car park wasn't empty, but it wasn't rush hour either. Despite the clunking echo of a couple dragging suitcases toward the terminal, the night was quiet.

Jethro climbed off the bike. Once standing, he rolled his neck, rubbing the cord of muscle with a strong hand. His eyes latched onto mine. They looked darker, more autumn leaf than precious metal, but still as cold.

I glowered back, hoping my hatred was visible.

His face remained closed off—not rising to the challenge of a staring war. Holding out his palm, he waited. The way he watched spoke volumes. He didn't wonder if I'd take his hand. He *knew*. He believed in himself so damn much everything other than his wish was dismissed as ludicrous.

Too bad for him, I didn't do well with the silent treatment. V had trained that out of me. Having a boisterous twin armed me with certain skills. And ignoring moody males was one of them.

Swatting his hand, I pushed off from the black leather and landed on bare feet. The brisk concrete bit into my soles. Wrapping my arms around my shivering torso, I muttered, "As if I'd accept your help. After everything you've done so far."

Dropping his arm, he chuckled. "So far?" He leaned closer. "I've done nothing. Not yet. Wait until you're in my domain and behind closed doors. Then you might have something worthy of being melodramatic about."

My skills at coping with the future rested on being able to ignore his threats and focus on the now. Standing tall, I said, "I could ask something stupid like why are we at the airport, but I can guess why. However, you failed to think about my schedule—"

"Schedules change."

"I don't travel alone, Mr. Hawk. I had tickets booked for my brother, assistant, and wardrobe organiser. Not to mention the excess luggage. They'll be expecting me. Hell, my assistant will be expecting me back at the hotel tonight. All of this—it's a waste of time. It's a waste because the police will be told and if you think my father won't come for me, you're mistaken."

Even as I said it doubt crept over my soul. Tex Weaver shoved me into this nightmare. Why did I think he'd come and bring me home?

Jethro crossed his arms, lips in a tight smile as if I were amusing and not pointing out valid facts. "There were a multitude of mistakes in that paragraph, but I'll focus only on the relevant points." Tilting his head, he continued, "Your father is fully aware of everything. Your loyalty to the man who gave you away with no fight is misplaced. His hands are tied and he damn well knows it. As for the police, they have no relevance in your future. Forget about them, your family, *hope*. It's over."

His voice dropped to a growl. "Do you know *why* it's over? It's over because your *life* is over. There's so much you don't know, and so much I can't wait to tell you."

He shed his icy exterior, grabbing my hair and jerking my head back. "You'll learn about your peerage. Your rotten family tree. And you'll pay. So shut up, give up, and appreciate my kindness thus far because I'm running low on decency, Ms. Weaver, and you won't like me when I hit my limit."

My shivers evolved to full blown tremors. "I don't like you now, let alone in the future. Let me go."

He surprised me by stepping away, releasing me. My scalp

smarted, but I refused to rub my head.

"You're testing me. But lucky for you, I know how to deal with troublesome pets."

Pets?

My hands balled.

How did I ever think I wanted him? The fact his lips had been on my face and his thumb in my mouth repulsed me.

Jethro's gaze drifted down my state of undress. "You're shaking. I don't want you getting sick." His eyebrow quirked. "I'd offer you my jacket, like the chivalrous man I am, but I doubt you'd accept it. However, I have something better."

Spinning around, he drifted toward a deep shadow cast by one of the large pillars. "Flaw? Get out here. You damn well better be—"

"I'm here." A man appeared from the shadows. Dressed in black jeans, shirt, and black leather jacket, the only glint of colour came from a simple silver outline of a diamond engraved on the front pocket. He looked like a thief waiting for a victim. "Been here for forty-five minutes. You're late." He tossed Jethro a duffel, running a hand through long dark hair. "Lucky for you the flight's delayed."

Jethro caught the bag, glaring at the man. "Don't forget your place. I'm not late according to my rules—not yours." Manhandling the duffel, he said, "You did as I asked?"

The man nodded. "Everything. Including photographic evidence. It all went smoothly, and the tickets are inside. I'll take care of the bike, just leave it there. Cushion and Fracture are tracking the Weaver men until you tell them otherwise."

Jethro pulled out an envelope, then flicked through the contents. He looked up, something resembling a smile gracing his lips. "Good work. I'll see you back at Hawksridge."

My ears pricked at the name. It sounded familiar—reeking of old money.

He's from nobility? The concept of Jethro being a duke or an earl was preposterous, and yet…uncannily perfect. Everything about him was deceptive and…bored. Was that all this was? A game to pass the time for some rich brat who got sick of killing puppies?

I couldn't stop my teeth from chattering—both from disgust and cold. The man named Flaw glanced my way. His eyes narrowed. "He's expecting you and the woman. I'll message and let him know it's gone well."

"Don't," Jethro snapped. His English accent thickened with the demand. "He doesn't need to know. He'll see us soon enough." Dismissing the man as if he was the hired help and no longer required, Jethro stalked toward me, holding out the bag.

Flaw dissolved back into the shadows like a scary apparition.

"This is yours. Get dressed. You won't be allowed in the building half-naked and shoeless."

Taking the duffel, I muttered under my breath, "I was dressed in an outfit worth thousands of pounds before you tore it off me."

I had two wishes—one, that he'd heard me and knew just how pissed I was. And two, that he didn't hear, because I was afraid of his reaction.

Jethro smirked before turning to his bike.

I opened the bag and promptly dropped it.

Oh, my God. I had to be dreaming. *Wake up, Nila. Please, wake up.*

My knees buckled, following the bag to the floor. Shaking, I collected the photos sitting on top of a mound of clothes. *My* clothes. Everything I'd brought to Milan—minus the fashion show apparel and my work tools—running gear, a bikini, sweat pants, pyjamas, and a simple collection of blouses, jeans, and maxi dresses.

But on top of it all rested strewn photographs.

Photo-shopped images that never happened.

Doctored snap-shots of lies. Such horrible, horrible lies.

No one will come.

Jethro was right. The police would laugh if anyone asked

for their help. What I held cemented my new life being Jethro's plaything.

Shuffling through the deck, I couldn't stop a hot tear searing down my cheek.

There was me—smiling, glowing. I remembered the day. V and I had headed to Paris for a local mid-season show a few years ago. He'd beaten me at poker in a silly pub tournament and a patron snapped an image of us. Laughing, overly warm, arms wrapped around each other in sibling affection, we'd been so happy.

Only Vaughn didn't exist in this photo. The background had been amended to show a fancy restaurant while the man who clutched me was Jethro.

The smile on his face was the warmest I'd seen. His attire of open-neck black shirt and jeans made him look young, in love, and dashing.

I couldn't study it anymore. Flicking to another one, I slapped a hand over my mouth.

This one pictured my father and me. Or *had*. He'd splashed out for the annual staff retreat, and we'd gone on a one week cruise around the Mediterranean. We'd stood with the setting sun dancing on the orange tinted waves, dressed in loose fitting 'cruise wear' that I'd created only days before. I'd planted an adoring daughterly kiss on his scratchy face.

That kiss now belonged to Jethro.

The ship had been tweaked to show a luxury yacht rather than commercial liner. The sunset cast a different glow. Jethro stood broodily, staring into the camera with such an intense glare of sexual power, no one would disagree that there was chemistry and need between us. The way my body curved into his, the sweetness and trust I displayed, only helped confirm the illusion of a couple besotted with each other.

The photos wobbled in my hands; another tear stained the glossy deception.

I looked up, not caring my heart was ripped out and beating coldly on the car park floor. "How—" Gritting my teeth, I tried again. "Destroying my dress wasn't enough? You had to steal my past, too?" I held up a photograph of a half-naked Jethro holding my chin as he kissed me. That wasn't based on my dateless life, but it was so lifelike, so true, so incontestable.

How did they make it so realistic?

Jethro shook his head, rolling his eyes. Locking the bike, he pocketed the keys before turning to face me. Dropping to his haunches, he whispered, "I not only stole your past. I've already stolen your future." Never breaking eye contact, he tapped the photographs in my hands. "You didn't see them all. Flick to the back. They're especially for you."

I couldn't unglue my lungs. I didn't think I'd ever be able to breathe without pain again. Splitting the tower of pictures, I glanced at the last ones. Immediately, I looked up. All sense of decency and pride gone.

"Please, you can't. This—it will break their hearts."

Tears scalded the back of my throat. My eyes burned, glancing down again. This one showed my empty hotel room—exactly as I left it with last minute ribbon and feathers littering the bed before rushing to the show—but now my toiletries from my nightstand, my laptop, and belongs were gone. Including my carry on and suitcase.

The room was abandoned. It looked as if I'd packed up and left my dreams, livelihood, and family without so much as a backward glance.

This would break my brother and father's heart, because it was the exact same way of how my mother, Emma Weaver, left us.

But unlike my mother, there was a simple note placed upon the dresser.

"Turn it over. I took the liberty of asking for a close-up, so you can read what you wrote as your final goodbye," Jethro murmured, stealing the photo from my fingers and tapping the fresh one revealed beneath it.

I curled over my knees, cradling the glossy replica of a

goodbye letter penned in my hand. The writing was exactly like mine, even I couldn't tell the forged sweeps and cursive from reality.

It's time I came clean.
I've been lying to you for a while now.
I've fallen in love and decided that my life is better with him. I'm done with the deadlines and unachievable pressure placed on me by this family.
I know what I'm doing.
Don't try and find me.
Nila.

I looked up. My heart collided with my ribcage, bruising, hurting. So much pain. I couldn't contain the sorrow when I thought of V reading this. To be left behind by both his mother and sister....

"They won't believe this. They know me better than anyone. They know I wasn't in a relationship. You said Tex knows all about you and why you're doing this. Please—"

Jethro laughed. "It's not for your family, Ms. Weaver. It's for the press. It's for the world stage who will make this fiction a reality. Your brother will find out the truth from your father, I'm sure. And if they behave, they'll both remain untouched. Believe me, this isn't to hurt them—if I wanted that, I have much better means." He cupped my cheek, brushing away long strands of my hair. "No. This was just an insurance policy."

"For what?" I breathed.

"So no one believes your family when they break and try to find you. They'll be all alone. Just like you. Controlled by the Hawks who've owned the Weavers for almost six hundred years."

Six hundred years?

"But..."

Jethro sniffed, his temper building like a ghost around us. "Stop crying. The images portray the truth. It proves you did what you did and no one can be angry or distrustful."

"What did I do?"

"Ah, Ms. Weaver, don't let shock steal your intelligence. You. Left. Voluntarily." He waved at the photo. "This confirms it."

"But I didn't," I whimpered. "I didn't leave—"

Jethro tensed. "Don't forget so soon what I taught you. You are the *sacrifice* and you..." His eyes dared me to finish his sentence, to admit to everything I'd done by protecting my family. His fingers twitched between his legs, looking like he wanted to strike.

I'd never been good at confrontation—not that my father yelled often or Vaughn and I argued. I'd grown up with no need to fight. I knew how precious my family was. My mother left, proving just how heartless someone could be if they didn't hold onto love. So I'd held on with both hands, feet, every part of me. Only to have it torn away so easily.

You'd rather they lived and never saw them again than die because of you.

Hanging my head, I murmured, "A sacrifice comes of their own free will. Therefore, I left voluntarily."

Jethro nodded, patting my thigh like the pet he thought I was. Covering the photos with his large hand, he pressed down until my elbows gave out and I lowered them. "Good girl. Keep behaving and the next part won't be too hard to bear."

Another rush of tears suffocated me, but I swallowed them back. He'd told me to stop crying. So I would.

Jethro stood, reaching down to scoop up the awful photos and duffel bag of belongings. "Come. We have to go." He didn't offer me his hand to climb to my feet.

The simple act of raising myself from cold concrete to freezing air taxed my already fractured world. Rolling vertigo pitched my balance, sending me reeling backward. My arms shot out, searching for something to grab hold of.

With drunken eyes, I begged Jethro to catch me, but he just stood there. Silent. Exasperated. He let me trip and fall.

I cried out as I collapsed on the ground. My fingernails dug into the rough flooring, holding on while the parking garage danced around like a nightmarish carrousel. Pain radiated from my hipbone, but it was nothing compared to the overwhelming nausea.

Stress.

It wouldn't be Jethro who ended up killing me, but the inability to deal with a gauntlet of emotions.

Closing my eyes, I repeated Vaughn's silly nursery rhyme. *Find an anchor. Hold on tight. Do this and you'll be alright.*

"Get up, goddammit. Stop acting the victim." A pinching hand grabbed under my arm, jerking me to my feet.

I doubled over, holding my stomach as another wave of sickness threatened to evict the only food I'd had today—a luncheon prior to the rehearsal of the runway show.

"You're useless."

When the debilitating wave left, I glared up. "I'm not useless. I can't control it." Breathing hard, I begged, "Please, let me talk to my brother. Let me tell him—"

"Tell him what? That you're being taken against your will?" Jethro chuckled. "By the look on your face you seem to think I'll forbid you having any outside communication—cut you off from everything you hold dear." Letting me go, he scooped my heavy hair from my neck, giving me a reprieve from the sticky heat of not feeling well. "Contrary to what you think, I have no desire to dictate what you can and can't do."

Twisting my hair, tugging lightly, he added, "This may surprise you, seeing as you have such a low opinion of me, but you can go online, keep your mobile—even continue to work if you wish. I told you before—this is not a kidnapping. It's a debt. And until you understand the full complications of the debt, I suggest you keep what's happening to yourself."

I couldn't understand. I was being stolen, yet was allowed access to avenues that could bring me safety. It didn't make sense.

"You've made a decision to come with me, and it's

irreversible. You can't change your mind, and you can't change the payments required, so why make others worry on your behalf?" His eyes glinted. "I suggest you become good at pretending if you wish to maintain the pretence of freedom. But I won't stop you from creating extra worry and strain for yourself." Bowing over me, he smiled. "It only makes my job easier."

Grabbing the black rope he'd made from my hair, I stepped away from him. "You're insane."

He gave me a sideways look, rummaging in the duffel to grab a handful of clothes. Closing the distance between us, he shoved the balled items into my stomach.

Oxygen exploded from my lungs from the force.

Jethro pulsed with anger. "That's twice you've questioned my mental state, Ms. Weaver. Do. Not. Do. It. Again." Running a hand through his hair, he growled, "Now get dressed. Time to go home."

Jethro

I COULDN'T DO it.

It was like looking after a needy, sickly, disobedient child. Bryan Hawk, my father and orchestrator of this mess, assured me it would be a simple matter of a few threats and blackmail.

She'll come easy if you threaten the ones she loves.

Bullshit.

The so-called inexperienced dressmaker had her own agenda. Beneath the chaste little girl, lurked a devious woman who was so tangled and confused she was fucking dangerous.

Dangerous because she was unpredictable. Unpredictable because she didn't know herself.

I was clueless on how to control her. I didn't understand her.

For instance, what the fuck happened at the coffee shop? She'd gravitated toward me. She'd licked my thumb like she imagined it was my dick. She'd *surprised* me. And I didn't do well with surprises.

My structured world—my rules and agendas—were not something that had room for twists and turns. Unless I was the one creating them. And I definitely didn't have time for my cock to twitch and show an interest in the woman I meant to torture and defile.

I would get hard when she was alone on my estate. I

would come with her gagged and subdued, hating me with the intensity of her forefathers.

Her pain was my reward. The fact she got me hard by being shy but so bloody tempting was completely unpermitted.

I checked my watch. The plane was due to leave in thirty minutes. *Do it. You know you want to.*

I couldn't stomach her presence any longer. I couldn't answer any more of her idiotic questions, or pretend I wasn't raging to teach her a lesson. Her tripping and stumbling got on my nerves. Not to mention her blind love toward a family that no longer had any right to her.

She needed discipline, and she needed it now. *Your hands are bound until you get her home.*

If I had to listen to one more beg or witness another tear, I'd end up killing her just to shut up her loud emotions.

Nila craned her neck, trying to read the boarding passes in my hands. Flaw, my right hand man and secretary to the Black Diamonds brotherhood, had already checked us in. Along with dealing with shipping my new purchase, the Harley-Davidson, and staging the runaway scene at Nila's hotel.

In precisely six hours, a housekeeper would find the photos, notes, and abandoned items, then the gossip columns would spread the story like a well incubated disease.

Nila Weaver's found love.

Nila dispels rumours she's in love with her twin by running off with some unknown English aristocrat.

My lips quirked at that. Me? An aristocrat?

If only they knew my upbringing. My history. If only Nila's father had spent the years he'd had with her preparing her for this day—informing her of our shared heritage, then perhaps she wouldn't look so fucking ill.

I'd told her the truth. Vaughn and Archibald Weaver were under strict monitoring. If they obeyed and went along with the ruse of Nila leaving for love, all would be harmonious.

If they didn't—well, the Weaver line would be snuffed out with the aid of a silenced pistol. And we didn't want that. After all, if there were no more Weavers, who would the Hawks rein over? Who would continue to pay the debt?

I looked at the woman destined to die for the mistakes of her ancestors.

She caught my eye. "Where are you taking me?" Her cheeks were colourless even though she had to be warm with the amount of layers she'd put on.

"I told you. Home." The word scratched across her face like carving knives. Home to me would be hell to her. I should've been more understanding—I could practically hear her heart shatter—but I'd been born into a family where emotion was a weakness. I prided myself on being strong, unbreakable. Empathy was the downfall of any human.

The ability to *feel* their pain. The nuisance of *living* their trauma.

That inconvenient ability had been beaten out of me as a child. Lesson after lesson until I embraced the cold.

The cold was emotionless. The cold was power.

Nila sniffed, striding a few steps away. Her curves were hidden in her new wardrobe of dark purple dress that came to her ankles, and a denim jacket. I hadn't permitted myself to truly look at her. She was skinny. Too skinny. But her black hair was thick and begged to be fisted.

Watching her dress in the parking garage irritated me. Her unsureness came across as coyness. Pulling the dress over her skirt was a reversed striptease. Her shaking fingertips had turned the ice in my blood into a lust I hadn't felt before.

It wouldn't take much to snap her petite frame. But despite her breakable body, her eyes gave a different story.

She ran deep.

I didn't bother caring how deep. But it did tempt in a way I hadn't expected.

A girl like Nila…well, that wasn't something to be broken lightly.

Her complexities, subtleties, depths, and secrets.

Each layer begged to be unwrapped and enjoyed.

Only once she stood before me, stripped bare of sanity and dreams, would she be ready.
Ready to pay her final debt.
Nila rubbed her cheek, displacing another silent tear. That single fucking tear stopped everything, freezing over the unwanted feeling of excitement at what my future held. Her sniffle gave me a layer of obligation rather than anticipation.
I wasn't going to, but she's given me no choice. Fuck it.
Moving closer, my hands opened to throttle her—to give her something to truly cry about, but I restrained myself.
She looked up, eyes glassy.
I forced a smile—a half-smile, letting her believe her tears affected me, offering false humanity. I let her believe I had a soul and didn't punish her for hoping. Hoping I was redeemable.
She bought it. Stupid girl. Allowing me to offer my arm as if it were some sort of consolation and guide her from purgatory into hell.

Nila

THE AIRPORT BAR reeked of sad goodbyes and tears. *Just like my soul.*

I rolled my eyes. I didn't like the sort of person Jethro made me. Someone who only saw the negative and was ruled by fear. *I'm an award winning designer. I'm wealthy in my own right.*

The unknown future crushed my heart, but it was the thought of losing myself while it happened that scared me the most.

"I need a drink. I'll get you one, too," Jethro muttered.

I spun to face him. Big mistake. I stumbled to the left, cursing the suddenly tilting room. My vertigo wasn't normally this bad. An episode a day was my norm, not every time I tried to move.

A cold hand grasped my elbow. "That condition you have—it's really getting on my nerves."

The floor steadied beneath my feet; I tore my arm from his hold. "Leave me alone then. Get on the plane and let me fall over in peace."

He shook his head, gold eyes darkening with impatience. "I have a much better idea."

I looked away, taking in the low square-line sofas, sad plastic plants, and dirty carpeting. *This can't be happening.* Everything seemed surreal. I was at the airport with a man who'd threatened the lives of my brother and father. I was about to climb on a plane with him. I was about to *disappear*.

And probably never be found.

It wasn't rational. It was completely nonsensical.

Suddenly, a drink sounded perfect. Alcohol and vertigo didn't mix, but damned if I wanted to exist full of grief and horror.

Jethro motioned toward a booth by the window where large spotlights turned the black sea of tarmac into false daylight, casting a warm glow on sleeping jumbo jets ready to depart.

Not giving me a chance to say anything else, or to even relay my preference, he stalked away, beelining for the bar.

Quick. Now.

The moment he had his back to me, I pulled my cell phone from my jacket pocket. He said I could keep it. He said I could talk to anyone I chose. He hadn't said when—now or when we got to his 'home', but I desperately needed Vaughn.

My eyes burned as I unlocked the screen. Hunching over the glowing device, I did as my captor ordered and made my way to the booth.

Typing in the number I knew by heart and practically the only number I ever called, I sucked in a breath.

A wall planted itself in my way.

A cold, unforgiving wall.

My head snapped up. Jethro crossed his arms, anger radiating from every inch. "What are you doing?"

I swallowed hard; my palms grew slippery with nervousness. "You said I could keep my phone. You said—"

"I know what I *said*. I may not stop you, but you still need permission. I am, after all, in control of your life from now on." Peering into my eyes, he added, "Don't make a rash decision you can't undo, Ms. Weaver." His English accent clipped my name in an unfamiliar way. He spoke it as if it were dirt. A filthy word contaminating his mouth.

My finger hovered over the call button for my twin. The

one man who I could say anything to and he would understand. Summoning what useless power I had, I said, "Please, may I make a phone call? I won't be stupid. I know what's on the line."

Jethro tutted under his breath. "That's the problem. You *don't* know. You think you do. You think all of this is a joke. You're not grasping the depth of what this means, nor will you until you've been educated."

Taking a step, closing the distance between us, he breathed, "But you do know one thing. You know what I will tolerate. Lying to me is another offence that comes with swift punishment. Stay honest, polite, and obedient and your heart will remain beating."

I wanted to scream at him. His quiet voice was worse than being yelled at. It was so…decent…so eloquent. It made all of this seem normal. And it so wasn't. So not normal.

"I understand. Do I have your permission?" My jaw ached I gritted so hard, refraining from what I really wanted to say. If I wasn't so afraid of this psycho I would hit him. I would leap onto his back and pummel him until he bled. Just to see if he *did* bleed, because a part of me expected him to be nothing but stone.

He frowned. "Fine. But I'll remain in earshot for this first conversation."

I shook my head. "No. I need privacy."

He smiled—a thin ribbon of emotion. "You need to realize privacy is a luxury you'll no longer have. Everything you do from now on will be monitored. Nothing will be hidden. Everything must be approved."

Everything? A horrible image of me begging to go to the bathroom only to be refused filled my mind. Not only had he taken me for something I didn't understand, he'd stolen my basic rights as a human.

I truly am a pet.

Jethro's hand whipped out, stealing my phone.

No! Being separated from it made all of this far too real.

The starkness of my situation hammered at my soul.

Staring at the screen, he scrolled rudely through my contacts. My very limited contacts. His eye twitched, handing the device back. "You seem to live in a world dominated by males. The only names in your preferred lists are men, aside from a mysterious entry Kite007." He stiffened. "Care to tell me if that person is female? I somehow doubt it, seeing as it's clearly a reference to the ridiculous James Bond Franchise."

Snatching the phone, I said, "I don't care to tell you anything. Leave me alone. I'm calling my brother. I gave you my word I wouldn't jeopardise whatever you're planning until I know the full story."

Jethro placed his hands into his pockets. His cream shirt and diamond pin were the epitome of class. In an ordinary circumstance, I would've been honoured and thrilled to have a date with a man with deliciously thick greying hair and a handsome face. I'd always preferred men over boys.

But he had to ruin it.

He ruined everything.

Jethro didn't move. Just stood there. Silently.

There was no winning. He wouldn't raise his voice or strike me to get his way—not in public anyway—but his posture intimidated me until I gave in.

Staring at the awaiting number, I deliberated against calling V. What did I hope to achieve? It would kill me to hear his voice. *But what if it's a lie and the moment he's got you where no one can see, he takes the only thing you have left?*

I couldn't risk it. Not if I could speak to V one last time.

Locking eyes with my gorgeously-groomed nemesis, I pressed the 'call' button and held the phone to my ear.

Being granted no privacy was horrid. My back stayed straight and all feelings of weakness were buried beneath false strength.

Do not cry. Do. Not. Cry.

The call connected on the first ring.

Vaughn never kept me waiting, almost as if he sensed it

was me calling—twin empathy connecting us once again.

Shit, what if he hears? What if he sensed my unhappiness? How would I stop him from coming for me—wherever I was going.

Vaughn's husky voice came down the line. "Nila. Tell me where you are. I'm coming to get you. Tex is acting really strange, and I'm done not being able to get a straight answer."

I sighed, turning my back on Jethro, staring at the airplanes below. So many things ran through my head. I wanted to ask how Dad was acting strange. What all of this meant. But I kept it all bottled up. For him. For them.

"I'm fine, V. I'm…"

I need you. Come get me. Save me please.

"You don't sound fine. Where are you?"

In hell with a monster.

Looking around the bar, I shrugged. "I'm exactly where I need to be."

To keep you safe.

"Stop with the bullshit, Threads. What's really going on?"

Sighing hard, I pressed a palm against my feverish forehead. I sucked at lying. Especially to V. "Something's come up. I'm going away for a little while. A holiday where I can unwind. I should be able to contact you—if the Wi-Fi and phone lines are good." I couldn't stop rambling. "Tonight really put a strain on me, you know? It came together so well, but it wasn't easy—you saw how bad it got toward the end. I just need—"

"What you need is a fucking spanking. You don't just leave without talking this through!" Vaughn paused, a disbelieving huff coming down the line. "You can't be serious. We had plans. You said you'd come with me when I went to Bangkok next week for more merchandise. We've booked the flights and everything."

I didn't want to be reminded of everything I was walking away from.

"I'm sorry, but I can't go. You have to trust me and not

push. Just accept what I'm telling you and that I need some alone time, okay? You'll be able to contact me by phone and email."

"This is bullshit."

"V, please. Be supportive, like you always are."

Don't make this ten times harder to say goodbye.

"Skype? I need to see you, Threads. Something doesn't feel right. You're keeping things from me."

A firm fingertip prodded my shoulder. Jethro whispered, "No Skype."

I didn't know how he heard V and didn't want to ask why Skype wasn't permitted. *Why doesn't he want my family to see me? Because who knows what you'll look like when he's finished.*

The fear I'd been able to keep leashed suddenly swamped me. I moved forward, collapsing into an uncomfortable booth.

"Threads. Threads?" Vaughn's voice echoed down the line. "Goddammit, Nila. What the fuck is going on?"

Sighing, I rested my elbows on the table. The weight of aloneness and depression settled heavily. "I don't know," I whispered.

The phone disappeared from my fingertips. "Hello, Mr. Weaver. We met earlier. Jethro Hawk." Jethro glowered, making me wish the seat would devour me.

A loud stream of curses came through the phone. Jethro pinched the bridge of his nose. "No, see that's where you're wrong. If you have an issue with me enjoying your sister for a time, speak to your father. For now, Nila is mine, and I won't have anyone saying differently."

He held the mobile away from his ear for a second while Vaughn exploded. A furious shadow darkened his face.

Jethro gripped the phone, growling like a rabid wolf. "That's none of your concern. I'm taking her. I've *already* taken her. And there's nothing you can do. Goodbye, Mr. Weaver. Don't make me regret my kind generosity toward your sister so soon."

He hung up, tossing me the useless phone. "If you want a

piece of advice on how to survive the coming months, don't talk to your brother again unless you want to pay a serious price. He's detrimental to your willingness to obey, and a fuckwit."

Tears welled. I didn't want to cry. Damned if I'd shed anymore useless liquid over this bastard.

"Don't call him a—" I stopped mid-sentence. There really wasn't any point in arguing. He'd win. Just like he'd won up till now without a curse uttered or shout yelled.

I'm meek. He was controlling me with no ropes or chains or curses. I was under his horrible spell, threatened by the illusion of him murdering the people I held most dear.

My eyes flickered toward the exit behind him. Jethro followed my gaze. He side-stepped, waving his arm toward the temptation of running. "You want to leave? Go. If you're so selfish to let others die for you, I'm not going to stop you. One phone call from me, Ms. Weaver, and it all ends for them."

I didn't move, deliberation a heavy cross on my shoulders. How could I sit there and let him take control of my life? But how could I ever live with myself if I ran?

He'd kill my family and there'd be nothing to run toward.

I hunched, deliberately looking away from the exit.

Jethro came closer, crowding me into the booth. "Good choice. Now sit there, don't move, and I'll get you something that'll make this easier." He turned away, but not before I heard his murmured, "For me at least."

I waited until he stood at the bar, smiling at the barmaid, before I opened a new message.

My hands shook, jiggling the phone, but I wouldn't stop. He might not let me talk to people I love, but people I hated didn't matter. The one person who drove me into this mess might be my only hope at surviving it.

If he forgave me.

Needle&Thread: *Kite, I don't do this lightly, but my life has taken a certain change and…well, I would like to be able to message you if it gets too much. I'm sorry I overstepped. I'm not going to say any more than…please. I need to be able to talk to you if I need to.*

I pressed send, hating myself and how weak I sounded. He wouldn't understand the strength and courage it'd taken to write that or bow into the meeker role. But I needed someone—a friend. And the sad part of my life was—I had none.

Resting my phone on the table, I stared unseeingly out of the window. Tears tried to take me hostage again, but I curled my hands, digging long nails into my palms. The pain gave me a distraction, letting me stay outwardly calm.

Jethro took his time, talking softly to the botoxed waitress. I wished he'd forget all about me so I could sneak out the door and never return.

My phone buzzed.

I'd never hoped for anything more in my life as I read the new message.

Kite007: *Understand me too when I say I don't forgive or forget lightly. But I appreciate your message and can't deny you've got me intrigued. You've almost got me wanting to know what changed in your life to send you grovelling back to me. I'm not an idiot to know it must've been pretty big after what we said to each other. I'll let you message me and reply on one condition.*

There was nothing else. Glancing over at Jethro, he had his back to me waiting for his order. Still time. Still hope.

I swiftly messaged Kite back.

Needle&Thread: *I accept. Whatever your condition.*

Please just give me someone to talk to. No matter how cryptic and shallow he was, I needed it. So much.

Kite007: *No details. I'll reply as long as your messages don't make me care. You've got the wrong man if you want sympathy.*

I wanted to tell him to piss off. That he wasn't worth it. But I swallowed my pride just as Jethro placed a single shot of white liquor in front of me. "Whoever you're messaging, stop."

Glaring into his light, unfeeling eyes, I flicked a curtain of hair over my shoulder.

In my first, but definitely not my last act of defiance, I

typed a single word.

One word that gave me a shallow friend who didn't care if I lived or died.

The only person I had left.

Needle&Thread: *Deal.*

Jethro

I TRIED.

If anyone asked, I could tell the truth. I did *try* to stay a gentleman.

But who the fuck was I kidding? My manners had an expiration date, and Nila pushed me too far.

I guided her from the dismal excuse of a bar, through the terminal, and past security. Her arm stayed looped with mine, following submissively, obediently—like a good pet. Her feet glided in flat shoes, her dark eyes glazed but aware.

It'd been too easy. Both breaking my word and dissolving the tablet into her drink. I said I wouldn't kidnap or drug her—that was before she showed some backbone in the coffee shop, and had the fucking audacity to ask me for something.

Sex? She willingly wanted some sort of meaningless connection with me? That pissed me off.

I'd been too soft. Too gentile. It was time to make my prey fully understand the nightmare she'd walked into and put a stop to the stupid fantasises she entertained.

And I couldn't think about her brother without wanting to fucking punch something. I shouldn't have been so lenient. I didn't care who she talked to as long as she remained mine to torment. But him—he could ruin everything. The Weaver men had been a constant pain in the arse since the Hawks started taking their women.

War had broken out. Lives were lost on both sides.

But we won. And would continue to win, because they were pussies and we were strong.

Nila didn't say a word as I guided her down the airbridge and onto the plane. To an outsider she looked perfectly normal. Perhaps a little tired and spaced out, but content and not in any way distressed.

That was the wonder of this particular drug.

Externally, she acted the perfect part. Internally, well....

It wasn't my problem if she saw everything that happened. Her mind was unhindered—loud and shouting—but all motor control was stolen. And there was nothing she could do about it. She dealt with vertigo on a daily basis—this was no different. I'd taken her ability with the help of a simple chemical. In fact, I was kinder than vertigo, because I gave her something to hold onto.

Patting her hand that rested on my forearm, I guided her into business class. Pointing at the window seat, I waited till she sat heavily, then buckled her in. Her breathing remained low and regular, but when I sat beside her, took her hand, and guided her face to mine, I saw the truth.

She knew.

Everything.

Perfect. It's time to begin.

Brushing black hair from her neck, I whispered, "I should warn you of something." Running my fingers down the silky strands, I moved closer so I could breathe the threat. Silence was terrifying. Whispers petrifying. But barely spoken threats were the worst.

"Be afraid of me, Ms. Weaver. Be afraid because your life is now mine and I'm the master of everything that happens to you. But know this...it's not just me you'll have to fear."

Her chest continued to rise and fall, no hiccup or flinch. But her eyes fought against the glass of unwilling intoxication, struggling to break the surface and no longer drown.

"There are others. Many others who have the right to help me ensure the debt is fully repaid. Ultimately they have to ask permission from me. But there are exceptions to every rule."

Settling back into the leather seat, I smiled. "Remember what I told you and you might survive."

My mouth said one thing, my eyes another.

Remember that and you'll still die.

She heard the truth as well as my lie. Her fingers twitched, mouth parted, but the drugs were stronger than her terror.

She was inert while inside she was screaming.

The silence was a screeching-symphony to my ears.

Nila

THE BLACK SUV that I'd been stuffed into at the airport rolled to a stop beneath a humongous archway. A gatehouse, so typical of large wealthy estates in England, soared above us. Through the glass roof of the car, I made out the same crest that emblazed the door panels of the vehicle I sat in. The up lighting made it glow like a rare monument—an over emblazed welcome doormat.

A huge filigree design with four hawks circling a nest of fallen women welcomed, complete with a large diamond glinting in the centre. It screamed of hunting and violence and winning.

I would've shuddered if I had the ability to move. How many of the fallen women lived through what I was about to? How many survived?

None of them.

I knew that now. I knew what my future held.

I'd screamed and raged and howled beside Jethro on the plane. My throat bled from shouting. My heart burst from begging. But he hadn't heard a whimper, because of the magic he'd used to subdue me.

The journey had torn my heart into shreds. Every step I took, I battled to break whatever spell he'd placed me under. Every breath I took, I fought to speak.

If I had the power of speech, I would've screamed that I had a bomb. I would've taken detainment and a full body strip search to flee from Jethro's undeniable, possessive hold.

My entire undoing and decimation was done in utter silence. And the bastard just sat there, holding my hand, nodding at the air-hostess when she said what an elegant couple we were.

He let me dissolve into misery. He lapped up my unshed tears, and I'd seen a glimpse of the monster I'd given my life to. Thousands of feet above the earth, I'd witnessed the cold gentleman mellow into something resembling a happy lover. Someone who'd won and got their way.

"Welcome home, Ms. Weaver," Jethro whispered against my ear.

I tried to cringe from his mouth, to huddle against the door, but the damn drug kept me locked beside him.

I blinked, inwardly sobbing, outwardly a perfect porcelain doll.

Everything had been stolen. My sense of touch, ability to speak, muscles needed to run.

A man in his early twenties appeared from a large pillar of the archway. Manifesting from the dark like a ghoul on Halloween. Jethro stiffened.

The new arrival opened the front door, sliding into the seat and nodding at the elderly man driving us. "Clive."

The driver nodded in return, gripping the gear stick with an arthritic hand, and engaging the car once again. He hadn't said a word since picking us up at Heathrow. *Perhaps he doesn't have a tongue? Jethro and his family probably ripped it out to protect their sadistic secrets.*

We inched forward, trading the soft lighting of a hawk engraved logo for the deep darkness of forest. I stared out the window into pitch black. From Italy to England, from night to night. The engine purred, following a quaint road slicing through dense woodland.

I wanted to run. And scream. I wanted so much to scream.

Jethro scowled as the newcomer twisted in his seat, awkwardly facing us. I struggled to make out his features thanks to the dark, but the high beams of the SUV cast shadows enough to see.

"Jet." He gave a mock salute.

Jethro sniffed. "Daniel."

"This her?" The man trailed his eyes from my lips to my breasts to my demurely placed hands in my lap. "She looks like a Weaver."

Jethro sighed, sounding bored and annoyed. "Obviously."

Daniel reached over, grabbing my knee. His touch sent shivers of repulsion over me, even through the cotton of my dress.

I felt that.

I held my breath. Sense of touch was the first sign of the drug wearing off. I knew when Jethro touched me, because of the pressure of his fingers. They acted like a punishment, a leash, and a reminder that my life was his. But up till now I hadn't been able to feel temperature or texture. Neither hot nor cold. Gentle or soft.

But now I could.

It's fading.

I hoped joy didn't show on my face. If I could move, I could escape. *Oh, Nila. Don't be so stupid.*

My joy fizzled out as fast as it'd arrived. There would be no escaping. It was yet another thing I knew just by what Jethro *wasn't* saying. I'd learned something in the short flight here. His silence told me more than any part of him. His silence shouted too loudly to be ignored.

I was dead already. My last breath hinged only on how quickly he tired of his new toy.

Keeping my emotions buried, I stared blankly at the man who dared touch me. His lips pulled into a cruel smile; his fingers tightened until every inch of me wanted to jerk away.

Jethro sat still, letting him touch me.

Daniel's nose was slightly crooked from a bad break, face

fuller, body softer than Jethro's, but there was no denying the family resemblance. Jethro was cold stone with sharp contours, gravelly voice, and imposing personality while the younger brother had more animation.

If it wasn't for the greed glowing in his eyes, I would've preferred him. But despite Jethro's granite exterior and sharpness, I knew in my heart I was better off being his plaything than this new Hawk.

There was something missing inside him.

A soul.

With a sneer, the man ran his palm up my inner thigh, bunching the material of my dress. "I must say you're very well behaved." He dug his nails into my delicate flesh, only a hand distance from my crotch. "You don't flinch." His hand suddenly left my thigh, connecting with a loud, stinging slap on my cheek. The force of his strike sent my useless body falling into Jethro. "You don't cry."

My face smarted and throbbed, making my heart race. I squeezed my eyes, wishing the sense of touch hadn't returned. I didn't want pain. I didn't want any of this.

Jethro grunted, pushing me upright with a rough shove to my shoulder. "She's not normally like this. Couldn't shut her up, or stop her endless questions. So I drugged her."

The man's eyebrow rose. "With what?" Eyes slithering over my chest, he planted his hand back on my leg. Pushing my dress out of the way, he inched higher and higher and *higher* on naked skin.

I wanted to curl into a ball and cry until I drowned from tears. I wanted oblivion from this nightmare. But the drugs kept me sitting prim and willing, a perfect toy to play with.

There are others. Many others who have the right to help me ensure the debt is fully repaid. The sentence had been on repeat in my head ever since Jethro whispered it on the plane. Was that why he permitted his brother to manhandle me? Would I be given to him to do as he pleased?

Please, God. Please don't let that happen.

I had enough strength to stay true to myself and survive one man. But multiple? They'd tear me into smithereens and ruin me even for death.

Jethro placed his hand—slightly larger and far more scary—on my other leg, pressing me hard against the leather. His touch hurt—burning my exposed skin like dry-ice. "I gave her Diamond Dust."

Daniel's vile touch stopped just as the tips of his fingers brushed the crotch of my knickers. I sat frozen, every part of me humming with horror.

"Diamond Dust? Shit, Jet, that stuff hasn't finished testing. You know Cut didn't authorise it to be sold yet—let alone be used in public. What if she had a seizure? How would you have explained she's nothing and deserved to die? You couldn't. You'd end up in fucking prison."

My heart hammered. Not only had he stolen my mobility, he'd run the risk of killing me. The fear crested again, burning through the drugs bit by bit. Even with the knowledge that I'd have to live through countless horrors before my time was up, I was glad I hadn't had a seizure. Death was so final. As long as I breathed, I *might* find some way to survive.

You say that now. My pain threshold hadn't been tested. I had no guide on how strong I'd remain or how precious my life would be when I no longer wished to live it.

Jethro shrugged. "If she died then the final debt would've been paid sooner rather than later." Glancing at me, he added, "I admit it's taking longer than I thought to leave her system. But it did a nice job shutting her up."

His fingers turned to pincers. "See how enjoyable silence is, Ms. Weaver?"

I stayed immobile beneath his touch, but my heart flew with terror, burning off the residual frozenness, leaving me at the mercy of reactions. Every second the drug weakened only meant I had to work extra hard to maintain the deception I was still its prisoner.

Daniel's fingers inched further. His eyes locked on mine as

he touched my clit through my knickers. His touch was horribly warm, invasive, and gross.

I wanted to kick him in the damn nose.

But I just sat there.

And died a little.

I sat there, because I had no damn choice.

Don't. I swallowed, drinking the tears fighting so hard to be shed. *Don't spiral.* I couldn't let myself be sucked into useless sadness. I'd never claw my way out. I'd never be ready to fight.

And I mean to.

My life might be earmarked for extinction, but I meant to be the last Weaver the Hawks ever took.

At least I don't have children. Once they killed me, there'd be no more Weaver women.

Oh, my God. Until Vaughn has children.

The fist around my heart squeezed until lightheadedness made the car swim.

Daniel yanked me from my horror, rubbing my clit. He grinned. "She looks younger than twenty-four. Sure you didn't get the younger sister instead?"

What!?

I jolted, sucking in a breath. I forgot to pretend the drugs still held me prisoner. A sister? Impossible.

She left us. Could my mother have had another life—a whole other existence that I didn't know about?

The thought pulverized my heart. Not only did she have a family—tearing us apart when the debt came for her—but she'd thoughtlessly given life to another girl?

Jethro's head snapped toward me, his light-brown eyes flashing in the darkness. I stayed as statuesque as possible. My gasp was the first sound I'd made since the bar. Since I entered into an agreement with Kite not to make him care, and the last conversation I had with my brother for who knew how long.

Jethro leaned into my neck. "I see you fighting it. I see you winning. You can't hide anything from me." Pulling away, his eyes narrowed. "You'd do well to remember that. Don't give me a reason to hurt you so soon."

Looking to his brother, he muttered, "She's the right one." His fingers clenched and unclenched on my thigh. In a lightning move, he snatched Daniel's wrist and jerked his probing fingers from my core. "She's the right one and *mine*. Enough."

I couldn't stop the sigh of relief. Only one other man had touched me there. Only one boy had seen me naked and taken my virginity. I never thought I'd be in a situation where I'd be forced, and for a fraction of a second I was grateful toward Jethro for stopping it.

"I can touch her if I want. Shit, I can fuck her too."

"I didn't say you couldn't. I just said…enough." He bit the word into pieces. Sharp, deadly, unforgiving.

Daniel tore his arm from Jethro's grip. "Fine. But don't climb up your arse thinking she's just yours. She's not. She belongs to all of us."

There are others. Many others who have the right to help me ensure the debt is fully repaid.

"No. But she's mine until I say you can have her. Hierarchy, little brother. You know how receiving charity works."

"Fuck off, Jet." Pointing a finger at Jethro's face, he said, "Cut changed a few things tonight at the Gemstone. He's named me VP—given me your role."

Jethro settled into the seat, his broad shoulders brushing mine. "If you think he did that behind my back, you're mistaken. I asked for time. Cut was more than happy to grant it. After all, I'm the firstborn son of a Hawk. She's the firstborn daughter of a Weaver. There are more important things on my agenda for the foreseeable future."

My brain swam. Everything they said sounded cryptic and layered in code. Cut? Was that a name? Gemstone? It sounded like a place, but that didn't make sense.

"You've always thought you're better than me. But you'll see who extracts a debt from flesh better when I get my turn."

Daniel sneered, his gaze bouncing from his brother to me.

I gritted my teeth against dropping my eyes or trying to turn invisible. As much as I hated Jethro, I would make sure to remain in his good graces as long as possible.

Daniel reached out and patted my knee, ignoring Jethro's icy look. "Enjoy your time with my brother, because when you're mine…enjoyment won't be something you'll be feeling."

Jethro sat forward, his suit rustling against the leather upholstery. In his signature terrifying quietness, he said, "You disturb my work before I'm through, blood or not, you'll pay the price."

The two men glowered. I didn't know either of them, but the air shimmered with past conflict and animosity—hinting that this standoff was nothing new.

"You're not untouchable," Daniel hissed. "You better—"

Jethro shook his head, eyes dark as amber. "Stop. There's nothing I better do. Father didn't pick you. He didn't *choose* you." His hand came up, casually checking his fingernails. "Life rewards those who deserve it. And you—don't."

Jethro was calm, made worse with the swirling ferocious temper existing just below the surface. The atmosphere thickened, changing the breathability of the car's interior until I choked with the urge to flee.

Clive, the driver, never slowed, continuing through the night as if brother rivalry and debts extracted from human misery was common. The gentle rocking of the vehicle did nothing to relieve the anger between Jethro and Daniel, but every wheel spin helped shed the fogginess I'd existed in for the past few hours.

The fact I was trapped between two males who might explode at any second helped drench my system in adrenaline, kick-starting my heart, dragging me to the surface of being master of my own body once again. The heavy drug-ocean receded.

I didn't witness what made Daniel concede—Jethro never moved—but he growled a curse, then spun in his seat to glare out the windscreen. I followed his attention, holding my breath at the soft glow in the distance. If that was our destination, it was giant. A looming residence breaking the darkness with false warmth and welcome.

My new home.
My new hell.
My end.

"It's called Hawksridge Hall. Take a good look, because it's the last place you'll ever live." Grabbing a handful of my hair, Jethro tugged me closer. His hot breath disappeared down my dress, making me tremble. "Hawksridge has been in our family for countless generations. A fortune we built from nothing. Unlike you, we weren't born into privilege. We earned our wealth. We deserved the titles bestowed, and it's time to show you what we had to do to achieve that."

His fingers wrapped tighter, burning my scalp. "To dispel any thought of running, there's over one thousand hectares of land. You'd never find your way to the boundary. You're trapped." His lips grazed over my jaw. "You're mine." Keeping his fingers tangled in my hair, he reclined, pulling my neck into an uncomfortable angle.

The sadness I'd done so well at battling crested again. There wouldn't be bars on my cage—or at least I didn't think so—but there was a fortified moat in the design of woodland and lakes and hills. I wasn't outdoorsy. I didn't know north from south.

But you do run.

I was fast. I had stamina. If the opportunity came, I wouldn't hesitate to put my obsession with running to use.

Until you fall and break your leg thanks to an episode.

My shoulders rolled. Not only was I trapped by a maniac family, but I was vertigo's favourite stumbler.

The car continued deeper and deeper. Every turn, I lost all sense of direction and knew I would never find the gatehouse without a miracle.

Taking a deep breath, I looked at my hands in my lap. I

willed sensation to come back. They twitched, returning to life with a wash of pins and needles.

They fell off my lap involuntary as we bounced over a cattle grate. Jethro pursed his lips, looking at my offending limb on the seat beside him. His gaze trailed up my arm to my chest. I breathed faster at the calculating look in his eyes.

Unwinding his fingers from my hair, he trailed them down my neck, along my clavicle, across my shoulder, and down my arm. "My brother was the first to touch you below, but I'm going to be the first to touch you here." His hand skated across to my breast, clamping around the sensitive tissue.

The soft cotton of my dress did nothing to protect me from the coldness of his grip.

"You seemed to want my attention at the café. Don't say I never give you anything." His finger pinched my nipple, rolling it painfully. There was nothing sexual about his hold—only punishment.

Giving up pretence of being under the influence of whatever he'd given me, I squeezed my eyes, swallowing back a whimper.

He twisted my nipple again, shifting from demeaning to the edge of painful, but what made it worse was I'd *wanted* him to touch me there. I would've willingly slept with him only hours before. Before I knew the animal inside the cultivated man.

"You're too skinny. I prefer women with more...assets than you," he whispered, cupping my other small breast. "However, your tiny stature might prove to be a blessing with some of the things I have planned." He pinched me again, turning my nipple like a corkscrew.

I flinched, forehead furrowing against the pain.

He chuckled. "I knew it was wearing off." His touch turned from painful to excruciating. I bit my lip, barely holding back a cry.

"Just in time." Letting my breast go, he captured my hand, linking his icy fingers through mine. There was nothing romantic or caring about Jethro holding my hand—it was a pure reminder that I had no chance in hell of getting free.

Vaughn. Tex.

I wanted so badly to talk to them. To beg for rescue. But I could no longer be the woman I'd been. I couldn't be the workaholic who blamed others for my unhappiness. I'd accepted my father's old-fashioned law about not being permitted to date, because in all honesty, I wasn't ready. I would never be ready. Because meeting someone meant the possibility of falling in love. Which meant the worst pain imaginable when they left.

If anything, Jethro had done me a favour. I never wanted male company again. If I could return to my sewing machines with no other companionship but my twin, I'd be happy, eternally grateful, and would live the rest of my life in peace.

Tugging my hand into his lap, Jethro murmured, "I meant what I said on the plane. Play your part and you'll live to see another sunrise."

Something snapped inside as if the drug suddenly gave up its hold on me, along with everything I'd been trying to avoid. The tears, the fears, the constant worrying of what was to come.

It all disappeared.

I couldn't afford to drain my energy with useless wonderings. Jethro said I could work. I intended to drown myself in fabric and continue designing my next runway show. I would pretend my world hadn't become a monster-filled nightmare, and lock my mind in a place where it was safe. Mundane was safe. Routine was safe.

I would create a sewing room deep in my soul and ensure no one—including the numerous activities Jethro had planned—could ever ruin me.

And talk to Kite.

My heart thumped. He wasn't kind or a sympathetic ear to cry to. But I was glad. I didn't want someone to pat my back and make me feel worse with commiseration. I needed someone to tell me to buck up, keep going, and never wallow in darkness.

Kite didn't know it yet, but I planned to use him as my barometer of liveliness. If I could muster up the energy to flirt and chat and pretend everything was okay, I had the strength to continue. The moment I used him as an outlet to purge whatever Jethro did to me, I would know I needed to re-centre myself and dig deeper to stay true.

Jethro let my hand go, tossing it away almost violently.

I breathed a sigh of relief, then stiffened as his fingers latched around my upper thigh.

Whispering harshly, he said, "Keep watching the horizon, Ms. Weaver. You're about to see your new home." His hand crept up my leg, following the same path his brother had—freezing my exposed skin with his icicle-like fingers. "Don't take your eyes off the windscreen. You behave and I'll make sure you have somewhere warm to sleep tonight. You disappoint me and you'll sleep with the dogs."

I bit my lip, eyes flaring wide.

Sleep in a kennel? *Shit, Nila. You couldn't be any more stupid.*

All this time I'd braced myself for sexual payments—bodily taxes and unwanted attention—but in reality I hadn't stopped to think about the bare essentials of living. There was so much more Jethro could do to me than torment my body.

He could deprive me of nutrition.

He could prevent me from sleeping.

He could make me live in squalor and suffer illness after illness.

Daniel stayed facing the front, ignoring us. I risked my first question since the airport bar.

"You aren't just going to use me. Are you?" My voice sounded strange after not speaking for so long.

Jethro stilled, his fingers twitching on my inner thigh. "So naïve. You're worse than a pet. You're like a child. A loveless girl who knows nothing of the big, bad world." Breathing shallow, his hand moved higher and higher. "Pity I'm not turned on by little girls. Pity you don't get me hard, my loveless, clueless Weaver. Then you might've been prisoner in my bed."

In front of us, the car's headlights illuminated a driveway. The woodland stopped, giving way from thicket to a huge expanse of manicured lawn and a large oval fountain. Birds of prey replaced angels and fair maidens, their talons dancing on top of water spray.

Jethro's hand burned, never stopping his slow assault. My heart jack-knifed, pain shooting in my chest as panic replaced my blood. I'd wanted sexual contact for so long but not like this. Not taken. Not even wanted.

The car slowed, skirting around the fountain. We turned left, following the sweeping driveway.

And that was when I saw it.

The monstrosity that was my so-called new home.

The rising monolithic, French turreted, tower fortified, sweeping, soaring mansion. Tarmac turned to gravel beneath the tyres, pinging against the metal panels below. Jethro's fingers crept higher, demanding I pay attention to everything he did.

"Welcome to Hawksridge Hall, Ms. Weaver. It's going to be a pleasure entertaining you as my guest." The sentence wrapped around me like a noose; my eyes snapped closed as his fingers brushed my core. Firm, unyielding, he cupped me through my knickers, sending snow to my womb with his vile fingers.

I bit my tongue, hating him. Hating myself. Hating everything to do with debts and vendettas and family feuds.

"This is what you wanted, isn't it?" Jethro whispered, pressing harder.

Everything clenched, repelling against his awful ministrations.

I tore my eyes open. "Not like this." Dropping my voice, I locked eyes with him. "Please, not like this."

The car rocked to a stop.

Daniel looked over his shoulder, his gaze dropping to the

blatant position of Jethro's hand between my legs. He smirked. "Welcome to the family. Don't know how much you've been told about us, but forget everything." His teeth glinted in the pooling light from the mansion. "We're much worse."

Jethro stroked me, drifting down to where the silk of my underwear gave a little, pressing against my entrance. "He's right. Much worse."

I shuddered as his finger bit into me. The unhurried, controlled way he touched me twisted with my mind. His violation was different than his brother's. Still not wanted, but at least more easily tolerated.

He was the devil I knew. Not the devil I didn't. In a morbid way, that made Jethro my ally rather than tormentor.

"I'll look forward till we meet again, Weaver." With another smirk, Daniel shoved open his door and disappeared.

Jethro's fingers rocked into me, but I refused to give him any reaction—neither upset nor regret. Sitting with my hands balled, I asked, "Why are you doing this?"

Jethro chuckled. "The ultimate question. And now that we're home, you're about to be told." Removing his hand, he opened the car door and climbed out.

All the blood in my body rushed between my legs—almost as if every molecule needed a cleansing—searching for relief from the hot, cold, tempting, *vile* way he'd touched me.

He looked so elegant in his dark grey suit, so refined with the glint of diamond on his lapel. Why did someone so horrid look so beautiful? It wasn't fair. Nature's cruel irony. In jungles, birds died from being attracted to the gleam of cavernous flowers. In rainforests, snakes and omnivores succumbed to toxin-riddled-jewelled frogs.

Beauty was the ultimate arsenal. Beauty was meant to deceive. It was meant to trick and beguile so their prey never saw death coming.

It worked.

And to a woman who made her life creating beauty for others and never being granted the ease of naturally acquiring it, Jethro was a double threat, both to my ego and lifespan.

Turning back to offer me his palm, Jethro waited for me to accept his token of help.

I ignored him.

I wasn't naturally a defiant person, but there was something about him that made me become a brat. Pushing off the seat, I propelled myself awkwardly and stiffly to the open door. The moment I was in grabbing distance, Jethro snatched my wrist and jerked me from the vehicle.

Of course, standing for me was already a careful affair, mixed with an unknown substance that'd hijacked my motor controls, I didn't land on my feet.

With a cry, I tripped out of the SUV, sprawling face first on the gravel below. The car suddenly cranked into gear and drove off. Leaving me alone and bruised before a manor worth millions.

"What on earth?" The gruff exclamation came from above—different from Jethro's deep timbre, but powerful and full of supple authority.

"Goddammit, this is getting ridiculous," Jethro muttered. "Are you going to be like this all the time?"

His strong hands lassoed around my waist, yanking me to my feet. The moment I was vertical I blinked, trying my hardest to find an anchor and remain standing. The world steadied and I shook Jethro's lingering hold off my hipbone. "Yes, I'm ridiculous. Yes, I've suffered all my life. Yes, I know it's a *huge* inconvenience for someone who wants to kill me that I'm already a little bit damaged, but did you stop to think—just once—that the reason I'm struggling more than normal is because of the stress you're loading my system with?

"Have you never dealt with an upset stomach or a tension headache?" Waving my hand in his face, I snapped, "It's the same thing. My body doesn't handle upsetting circumstances well. Get over it or let me the hell go!"

It felt wonderful to let go of the anger bubbling inside. It purged me a little, giving me room to breathe.

Jethro remained steadfast, his eyes wide, mouth thin and unamused.

"Well, she has fight. All the fun ones did."

The man who'd spoken stood on the second-to-last step of a humongous portico. The house loomed overhead, blotting out the moon and stars as if it were a living entity. Burnished copper gilded the many roofs and turrets, criss-crossing flowerbeds lived beneath soaring lead-light windows, and lattice planted grass grew on the side of the turrets. It wasn't just a building—it was alive. Maintained, proud, a piece of impressive architecture that had weathered centuries, but been so well cared for.

I craned my neck left and right. The building continued on and on, at least ten stories high, with intricate alcoves, sweeping doorways, and a hawk embellishing every keystone.

It's a work of art. I was a creator. My passion didn't just lie in textiles, but in everything where a level of skill blared from every inch.

And Hawksridge Hall was majestic.

I wanted to hate it. I despised the family who owned it. But I'd always been a lover of history. I'd always pictured myself as a lady of a manor, with horses and gardens and refined dinner parties. I loved exploring stately homes, not for the furniture or statues, but for the drapery, hand-stitched wallpaper, and massive hanging tapestries.

Jethro took a step toward the older gentleman. "You said it would be easy. I can assure you, it wasn't." Throwing a cold look over his shoulder, Jethro motioned me forward. "Come here and pay your respects."

I didn't move.

The older man chuckled. He wore all black, and just like the man who brought my belongings in the parking garage in Milan, he wore a black leather jacket with a silhouette of a diamond on the pocket.

His hair was fully white, yet his face wasn't too weathered. He had a goatee, which was more dirty grey than snow, and eyes were as light and unnerving as Jethro's.

Instantly my back stiffened; my heart bucked in refusal. This man didn't deserve respect. I wanted nothing to do with him.

Just as I knew the younger man in the car was Jethro's brother, I knew without a doubt this was his father. This man was responsible for upholding the evil pastime of torturing innocence for something that should stay in the past. He was ultimately responsible for my demise.

Jethro stalked back, stole my arm, and marched me forward. Under his breath, he said, "Don't annoy me. I'm warning you."

Jerking me to a halt in front of his father, he spoke louder. "Ms. Weaver, let me introduce you to Bryan Hawk. Head of our family, President to his fellow riders, and current man in a long line of succession to wear the family name."

He glared at me, making sure I listened. "He's also known as Cut amongst his brotherhood. But to you, he will always be addressed as Mr. Hawk."

Mr. Hawk grinned, holding out his hand. "Welcome to my humble abode."

I shied away, not wanting to touch him, be close to him, or even have to tolerate talking to him.

Jethro growled under his breath, grabbing my elbow and holding me firm. "You're one infraction away from sleeping with the hounds, Ms. Weaver. Try me. Disobey once more."

His father laughed. "Ah, I remember those days. The fun, the discipline." Climbing down the final step, he closed the space between us. His aftershave reeked of sadism and old money—if that had a smell. A horrid mix of spice and musk that gave me an instant headache, whilst his eyes stole everything about me from my reflection to my dismal future.

He cupped my cheek.

I flinched, expecting the brutality and roughness I'd come to expect from a Hawk, but he ran his thumb gently over my cheekbone. "Hello, Nila. It's a pleasure to once again entertain a Weaver in our modest home."

Hearing my name repulsed me. Jethro hadn't used it yet—sticking to the impersonal address of my last-name. I hated that Mr. Hawk thought he had the authority to speak it.

Wanting to spit in his face, I focused on the house behind him—swallowing the urge. My gaze soared to the stained glass windows, the imposing spires, and impressive stonework. There was nothing modest about this dwelling, and he knew it.

I kept my lips clamped. I had a whole novel of horrible things I wanted to say, but Jethro's seething bulk beside me kept my tongue in check.

Jethro let me go, pushing me into his father. "She's been nothing but trouble. I can't deny I'm looking forward to tomorrow."

My heart leapt into my throat at the dark promise in his voice. *What's going to happen tomorrow?*

Mr. Hawk dropped his palm from my cheek, wrapping his arm around my waist. With his free hand, he brushed wayward strands from my eye. "You look just like your mother. It's a pity I'm not the one extracting in this particular instance, but rest assured, I will enjoy you once or twice."

My stomach latched onto my heart, making me sick. *Don't ask*. The question blared in my head. *What did you do to my mother?*

I'd been so young and full of righteous anger at her leaving my father. I thought she was the villain—the heartbreaker.

But she was the one who paid an unpayable price. And never returned.

Mr. Hawk's eyes glinted. "I see Jethro hasn't told you anything yet." Trailing his hand from my hair to my lips, he stroked me gently. "That's going to be a fun conversation, but for now I'll let you in on a little family secret." Crushing me against him, he whispered, "I'm the one who stole her. I'm the one who took debt after debt from her unwilling skin. And do you know what she begged for in her final minutes of life?"

My head swam. My world roared. Life as I knew it ended.

I hated him.
I loathed him.
I'll kill you.
I'd never felt such heat, such insanely burning desire to cause harm. My teeth ached from clenching; my nails drew blood from my palms.

"She begged for your life. To end it with her and to let you live in peace." His hand left my waist, grabbing my arse with a vicious grip. "Know what I told her?" His breath smelled of liquor and cigars, making me swallow his words. "I told her you were born a Weaver, you'll die a Weaver. And that's the simplistic way of our world."

Shoving me away, I ping-ponged from father to son, coming to an abrupt halt in Jethro's arms. The relief at being away from the man who'd murdered my mother made my limbs weak and jittery, but I couldn't stop the hatred from gnawing a gaping hole in my soul. I needed it out. I needed it spoken so he would know the debt might not have ended with my mother but it would end with me.

It will.

"I pity you. I knew nothing about you, your sons, your warped perception of life until tonight. I may not know why you're doing this but I do know one thing. I know that it's the last time you'll ever do it."

"Quiet!" Jethro shook me. But I wasn't scared of him. I wasn't scared of any of them anymore. They were bullies. Sadistic bastards who'd met their match.

Struggling in his arms, I freed my hand, pointing a livid finger at Mr. Hawk. I lost my rage, tilting head first into lunacy. My temper gave me power over everything. My cursed balance. My sheltered beginnings. In that one moment of brazenness, I found a nucleus of strength I didn't know I had.

My voice pitched as I yelled, "I'll kill you! I'll watch you die just like you watched my mother—I'll kill you! You don't deserve to live. I'll kill you and—" I launched myself at him, only to stumble and go slamming back against a powerful form.

Jethro grabbed my shaking arm, pinning it to my side. His strong hold crashed me against his body, moulding my wiggling behind against his rigid front.

His body was hard and firm—exactly like the stone I thought he was. The bulge in his trousers pressed against my lower spine.

"You've pushed me too far. You just had to fucking push. No one threatens my family, least of all a girl who can barely stand without support. And a Weaver." He spat on my feet. "Fucking filth."

"Remove her from my sight." Mr. Hawk sniffed. "Teach her her place, Jethro. I won't put up with such stupid behaviour." His eyes landed on me. "As for you. I'd hoped you'd show more promise. Think what you want of us, Ms. Weaver, but this isn't a simple matter that will end quickly. You're ours for however long we wish to keep you and you'll learn proper manners if we have to beat it into you."

Nodding at Jethro, he climbed the steps to the two-story-sized front door and disappeared.

The moment he vanished, my spine rolled and I wanted nothing more than to fall to my knees and cry.

What was I thinking?

My rage and hatred snuffed out like a candle in a storm. I'd never been so out of control. My emotions had held me hostage and I'd snapped—for the first time since my mother left—I'd succumbed to the intense freedom of bitterness.

Jethro dragged me backward, his dress shoes crunching against gravel. He didn't wait for me to back-peddle, just clutched me hard, dragging me like a corpse. "You've surprised me twice tonight, and I haven't liked either of them. You've pissed me off. So much so that—"

Slamming to a halt, he shoved my shoulder blades. "Get on your knees."

I wheeled forward, crashing from standing to landing on all fours.

No!

I winced as the driveway bit into my palms; my knees throbbed as sharp pebbles cut into my skin. I looked up, my face swollen and achy from unpermitted tears welling as deep as a bottomless lake.

This was the truth. This humiliation and admittance of power, not the farce he'd painted.

Jethro towered above, his legs planted wide, face etched in livid anger. "I'm a firm advocator of rewarding good behaviour but after tonight you've proven there is nothing to reward. You're wild, unwilling, and a spoiled brat who *will* learn her place."

Leaning down, he grabbed my long hair, jerking it hard. "Did you honestly think, after an outburst like that, that you'd deserve the comfort of a bed? Why do it, Ms. Weaver, when you knew what was on the line?"

I couldn't speak. My throat was pulled back, the pressure stopping all sounds and swallows.

"I have a good mind to fuck you right here. To smash whatever sense of entitlement or hope you're holding onto." He shook me.

My eyes watered at the pain.

"You're not hearing me. This is your life now. I am your only friend. Stop. Pissing. Me. Off."

You're not my friend. I have one, and his name isn't Jethro.
Kite.

I didn't think I'd want to message him so soon, but I needed someone from the outside world. I needed reminding that the universe hadn't entered an alternate dimension and there was still hope.

When I remained silent, Jethro snarled, "You're sleeping with the dogs. They have better obedience than you, perhaps you can learn from them on what we expect."

I sniffed, fighting so hard against tears.

I didn't even care that I wouldn't sleep in a bed. I was past worrying about sanitary conditions or nutritious food. All I wanted was freedom.

"Move," Jethro breathed, his beloved silence smoothing his outburst from before. "Don't make me show you how a good dog moves."

He wants you to crawl.

It had begun.

This was the beginning. And I'd brought it upon myself.

He wants to destroy you.

Using my hair as the leash, Jethro paced beside me as I went from stationary to crawling. I crawled like an animal. I crawled like a pet. I crawled through manicured gardens, past ponds, and statues, all the way from manor to kennel.

Jethro

I STRETCHED, LOOKING up at my ceiling. The plasterwork around the huge chandelier never failed to let me know who I was.

A Hawk.

The intricate rosettes and architraving was a testament to my namesake. Birds of prey swooped, hunted, and devoured small animals from above.

My hard cock lay heavily against my stomach. My hands clenched beneath my head. I was so fucking close to breaking the rules and taking Nila last night. She'd pushed me too far. I'd wanted to see how smart her mouth could be with my dick jammed down her throat.

I should've taken her.

Removing my hand from beneath my pillow, I grasped my morning wood and stroked. My eyes snapped closed as I imagined a different outcome to last night.

Nila's pink plump lips opening. Me sliding inside her mouth. My balls tightening as her timid tongue welcomed my cock. She'd lick me just like she'd done my thumb. Eager, inexperienced—a novice with so much to give.

I'd rock forward, holding her head, giving her no choice but to take more of my length.

I'd thrust harder, driving her from accepting to choking.

Fuck.

My hand worked tight and fast. The large bed creaked as I arched my back, giving into the fantasy of blowing down Nila Weaver's throat.

Fuck, yes. Take it. Yes.

My quads tightened, and I groaned as the first spasm of release shot from my balls, creating a sticky mess on my stomach.

Fantasy Nila kept sucking me, drawing another wave of pleasure. I liked her a lot more with my cock in her mouth. She was silent. Incapacitated.

I shivered as the last spurt of my orgasm joined the mess. I opened my eyes.

"Goddammit." I hadn't meant to do that. *Fuck it. It was a long night.* I deserved a little…unwinding.

It's going to be an even longer day.

I might've blown my load with an imaginary vision of Nila on her knees, but it would soon become real. Today, Nila would be initiated. She'd be welcomed. And not just by me.

Swinging my legs out of bed, I prowled across the thick red carpet toward my private bathroom.

I smiled, perversely happy with the day's upcoming activities. The next few weeks weren't about debt repaying or vengeance, they were about hospitality and welcoming a new Weaver into the Hawk household. She had much to learn, her place to recognise, and all thoughts of who she was torn from her soul and burned.

I'd use her. My father would use her. My two younger brothers would use her. If I let myself, I would feel sorry for her.

But that permission had long since been beaten out of me.

After spending some time alone with her, I knew the handful she was. Despite her disobedience, I rather liked her fire. Pity that fire would snuff out almost instantly.

I paused, searching inside to see how strong my barricades were. To see if I had enough ice inside to do everything expected of me. She was pretty, I had to admit. She had a certain intrigue. But she was just a woman.

A woman who confuses you.

Scowling, I shoved the thought away. She confused me which wasn't a good thing. It was almost as bad as surprising me.

One moment she seemed so sure and strong. The next she was brittle and breakable. And her bloody vertigo was getting on my goddamn nerves.

No. I was more than happy to let my fellow brothers share the work in ruining her. It would be over faster, and I could go back to my life before I knew of the stupid scroll stained with the blood of the first Weaver debts.

The sun spilled like a golden carpet, leading the way from bed to shower. My room was vacant of personal touches but reeked in history of past owners. Rococo style dressers, Victorian designed chairs. The wallpaper was embossed maroon leather with gold accents.

The entire space was brooding and temperamental. I would've preferred clean lines. White—which was the silence of the colour palette—with stone furniture and metal chairs. I liked to be surrounded by an unfeeling atmosphere but I'd never be permitted to change this area.

It was sacred.

All because it'd been the bedroom of all Hawk men who'd inherited a Weaver woman. Their last breath was taken in this mansion. It held the ghosts of Nila's ancestors and would one day absorb hers, too.

The birthday present of new spurs and a heinously wicked whip glinted on the eighteenth century sideboard. At the time, I'd thought it was a piss poor present for turning twenty-nine, but the best present was due next year. The true inheritance I'd been waiting for. One much better than a woman or her tears. When I turned thirty, I would own it all.

Everything. All mine.

The fantastic ruling of Primogeniture meant as firstborn

son, I inherited the lot. My brothers wouldn't get penny. My sister not a single diamond. They would survive by my charity. Just like my father.

The brotherhood. The mines. The yachts. The cars. Hawksridge. And every property overseas.

Mine.

Bryan Hawk, Cut to those in the Black Diamond brotherhood, would be second to me. The way of our ancestors ensured young authority remained in control of an estate that'd spilled enough blood to fill a moat around our gates.

My father would retire, and I would be king.

I'd upgrade from living in the bachelor wing with its pool room, theatre, office, weaponry, solarium, six bedrooms, and six bathrooms to having the pick of a fifty room, two ballroom, and a dungeon-equipped house to play in.

And by play, I meant *rule*.

Collecting new clothing from my walk-in wardrobe, I glimpsed myself in the mirror. My lips curled in disgust at the sticky mess on my stomach. I had a good mind to get Nila and make her lick me clean.

That was her fault.

My mind drifted back to her—against my will. She'd not only taken up valuable space in my head, but my day's structure as well. There would be no hunting today or inspecting the latest diamond shipment.

There'd be no business or travel.

All my energy and focus belonged to the woman who was a waste of my time.

Another daydream of forcing her to her knees stopped me on the outskirts of the bathroom. Would she cry or scream as I fucked her from behind? Perhaps she'd surprise me again and moan in ecstasy. I planned on taking her that way—the animalistic way. After all, she did spend the night with the dogs. It would only be fitting.

Dumping my clothes on the vanity, I strode into the four-headed quartz shower. I had no need to strip. I slept naked.

Always did.

It was part of the rules.

Living at Hawksridge, the grandest and most exclusive motorcycle club compound in all of England, came with strict unbreakable rules. Our brotherhood was different. We were smart, cunning, focused.

Any man found sleeping with clothes on was in for a night of pain. We might have left the dark ages behind but my family upheld strictness.

We made our fortune in the most transferable precious item there was. And we'd learned a lot from past mistakes on how to treat those who tried to steal them.

No clothes at night and random cavity searches by day.

All to protect our legacy. The way we made our money. The way we rose from penniless thieves at the beck and call of the Weavers to gathering a wealth that morphed to obscene a few centuries ago.

Stepping into the shower, I turned on the hot spray. Smiling at the mirrored wall, I cupped my cock, washing the residue of my indiscretion.

The next time I come, I'll be inside the woman I inherited.

With my cock in my hand, I nodded at my reflection.

I'm a Hawk but blood doesn't flow in my veins. I'm born of a substance unbeatable by any other—diamonds.

I'm a smuggler.

I'm a dealer.

And I'm about to become...a killer.

Nila

NEEDLE&THREAD: *I'm warm and in bed. Surprisingly I slept better than I thought I would. Did you have a good night? Did you lie in your bed and picture me pleasuring you? What did I do to you? Tell me, Kite. I want you to transport me from reality and give me a fantasy stronger than my present humdrum life.*

Kite007: *Forward this morning, aren't we? You're that desperate to talk about my cock? Not that I'd ever say no—but I'm rather impressed. Tell me more…beg.*

Needle&Thread: *Beg? How does one beg for something they need rather than want? Would you prefer me on my knees? Or perhaps on my back ready for whatever you wanted to give me?*

Kite007: *Fuck. What's got into you? Beg. Imagine I'm standing over you with my hard cock in my hand. I'm throttling it—my fist working so fucking hard at the thought of you spread-eagled and fingering yourself. Give me a visual. Now. Then I might reward you.*

Needle&Thread: *I'm exactly as you said. Begging, whimpering, touching myself until my whimpers turn to pants and my begs turn to moans. I'm wet for you. I'm hot for you. Please, Kite. Give me my fantasy. Give me something warm to hold onto.*

Kite007: *What the fuck is this about? How can I come when you sound weird?*

Needle&Thread: *Weird? I'm not. I'm giving you what you want in return for what I need.*

Kite007: *Is that supposed to make sense, 'cause I don't understand bullshit code. Fuck, you're seriously making me do it.*

Needle&Thread: *Do what?*

Kite007: *Ask you! Okay, fine. What's got your panties so bunched that you're coming onto me so strong. What happened to my timid naughty nun? Why the fuck do you sound so different?*

I stared at my phone, heart rate skyrocketing. I'd tried to play it coy and courageous. I thought I'd pulled off the pantomime that I was still myself, still living my content but uninspiring life.

Obviously not.

I re-read my past replies, unable to see the difference. Had I changed that much already?

There was nothing soft about Kite. There was no reason for me to seek him out when I had enough bastard in my life thanks to Jethro. It made no sense to let him use me—but it did in a strange way. It made sense because I *willingly* gave him control over me—something I needed in my rapidly spinning out of control life. While Jethro was determined to undermine, throw away, and rule every inch of whatever little power I had left, Kite gave it back in some strange, wonderful way.

He's the monster I know. He's not sweetness and light—but he's mine because I choose *him to be.* The defiance was yet another stupid score against the beast called Jethro Hawk.

Straightening my back, I tried to figure out a way to possibly get Kite to soften—just a little.

Kite007: *Tell me, then make me come. You've got two jobs to do. Do them.*

Taking a deep breath, I opened a fresh message.

Needle&Thread: *Tell me if this is out of bounds, but in answer to your question—why do I sound different—I suppose it's because I* feel *different. Everything is different. I thought I'd always fight against different. I like normal. I like routine. I thought different would ruin me. But…then…I changed.*

Kite007: *Changed? You really going to make me drag this out? My cock is hard and balls want to come. Spill it, so we can get to the second*

123

part of your to-do list.

Needle&Thread: *I'm the one who's different now. It's as if everything I've been dealing with suddenly doesn't matter. It's just gone....*

Kite007: *Gone?*

Needle&Thread: *Yes. It's liberating, scary as hell, and confusing. But something's changing inside—it feels as if I'm...growing up.*

I sighed. He'd send something horrible back—my response had been too personal. I knew that. But I'd sent it anyway.

Kite007: *Out of bounds. Get back to the subject. Let's try this, here's something you obviously want: I'm happy you're growing up—makes me feel a lot fucking easier knowing I'm not jerking off to a kinky fourteen-year-old. And now for want I want: I'm done with the cryptic crap. Pay attention, because I'm sliding my cock into your mouth. You try to talk but you choke on my length, your voice is humming against my balls. Stop trying to communicate and settle in to your task. Suck me.*

I sighed. Two emotions swirled inside—exasperation and gratefulness. He'd replied to my overshare. He hadn't shot me down or been the pillock he usually was. Progress.

The tentative softness inside was enough to get me through the next few hours.

Shouldn't you want more?

My heart hardened.

Kite had replied to my veiled hints for encouragement but I'd hoped...

It doesn't matter what I hoped.

It seemed everything I wanted in this world wasn't available—including more than one kind word from Kite. We'd been so close to a normal conversation. Learning, sharing, building a connection despite the complications of sexting.

He'd let me in for a microsecond then shut me out once again, using sex as a tool to keep me in my place and remind me I didn't factor in his life. I was the unseen whore. The unpaid prostitute who lived in his phone.

I couldn't let him hurt me. I couldn't let him weaken me. He'd done what I needed—reminding me I was strong enough. There was nothing else to do but finish the conversation, so I could leave the soul-sucking fantasy and return to the tragedy of my new world.

Kite007: *You're not sucking. Fine, I'll give you some encouragement. If you blow me, I'll return the favour. I'll flip you onto your back, spread your legs, and bury my face between your legs. I'd bite you, fucking you with my tongue until you forgot everything and came.*

My stomach attempted a small swoop. It wasn't romantic, but it did give me a tiny bit more warmth I needed.

Before I could reply, another message vibrated.

Kite007: *Tell me where you are right now. Are you naked? Finger yourself for me. Take a photo if you're brave.*

I laughed. The sound shredded the space that Jethro had so kindly given me for the night. Laughing was the only thing I could do. Take a photo? Of *what*? The bruises on my palms from crawling to the kennels last night? How about the cuts on my knees?

Maybe he wants a picture of my elegant bedroom and wonderful bedfellows.

Looking up for the first time since I woke, I let the uselessness of my situation get the better of me. The bravery I'd been clutching to like a raft in a rolling ocean, splintered and drowned. Painful despair saturated my heart, weighing me down like the anchors I so often clung to.

By all standards, the kennel was sheer luxury. The roof was watertight. The floor clean and sanitary. It was even draft free.

But it wasn't just mine. I had to share.

Squirrel, my favourite of the eleven canines I'd spent the night with, nudged my arm. I'd named him after the tree-climbing rodent thanks to his slightly bushy tail. With a doggy smile, he wheedled his way under my arm, leaning heavily against my torso.

I'd never had pets growing up. As a family, we were too busy working or travelling to exotic places to source more material and merchandise. Until last night, I'd had an adolescent fear of dogs.

That had evolved to terror when Jethro threw me inside.

I shuddered, hugging Squirrel closer to me, stealing his gentle warmth. Last night Jethro had tried to destroy me. Not through fists or rape or even harsh words. No, he tried to destroy me by removing any entitlement I had as a human. Marking me as no better than the dogs he kept.

He would've succeeded if my terror hadn't mellowed into bewilderment then gratefulness. He'd done me a favour—I preferred the company of his hounds. They not only tolerated my intrusion but welcomed me into the pack.

Squirrel licked my pebble-indented palm, letting me know he understood my aches. I still suffered from crawling from the manor, past immaculate flower beds, over precision mowed grass, and cutting through shadows cast by imposing hedges.

Everything throbbed when I finally crawled the last metre and sat waiting beside a large roller door. My dress was torn, my knees bleeding—not that he'd cared.

The estate was bigger than I could contemplate, but even in the darkness, I'd made out the buildings around us. The stables were across the cobblestone yard. A granary let its soft grainy fragrance permeate the air. The gentle huffing of horses broke the silence along with wuffles and snuffles from dogs.

Jethro left me sitting on my knees while he disappeared into what I assumed was a tack room. He returned with a large scratchy blanket and a bucket, before unlocking the roller door and beckoning me inside.

Throwing the items into the dark interior, he bowed. "Your boudoir, my lady." Leaning down, he swatted my behind. "Go to bed like a good little pet. You have a big day ahead of you."

When I didn't move, his foot landed on my arse, shoving me forward, giving me no choice but to crawl quickly into darkness.

The moment I'd traded starlight for no light, I panicked.

Jethro threw the bolt home, locking me inside a room that

thrived with moving bodies, claws on cobblestones, and soft growls of ownership.

The first brush of a wet nose on my cheek ripped a small scream from my lips. I curled tight into a ball, hugging my knees, squeezing my eyes against being eaten alive.

I waited for sharp teeth.

But they hadn't eaten me.

Far from it. I'd been licked and nuzzled and welcomed into a pack.

I was a stranger in their domain, but when I finally overrode my fear and looked into their eyes, they were bright with curiosity rather than territorial anger.

The rest of the night was spent making a semi-comfortable bed out of a loosely packed hay bale, and wrapping myself tight in the scratchy blanket. I'd aimed to sleep alone with my new friends scattered in their usual spaces, but they had other ideas.

Once I was settled, they'd crowded around me, squeezing close, curling around each other until I was the epicentre in a nest of canines.

The moment they'd quietened, I took out my phone.

Five missed calls, three messages from my twin, and one from my father.

Biting my lip to retain what composure I could, I'd read my father's first.

ArchTextile: *Nila, I know you'll have questions. I know you'll hate me. But please, my wonderful girl, know I didn't want any of this. I was stupid not to heed your mother's warning. I thought—well, it doesn't matter what I thought. I hope we can talk—when you're ready. I understand if you can never forgive me. I don't know how much of this they'll see, but I'll never stop searching, never stop hoping. Please don't think I gave you up lightly. They have...ways. They have you but they'll keep you in good health. We have time. Love you, sweetheart.*

I didn't want to focus on what time meant. The slow plod of time intertwined with the fast tick, tick, ticking of my final heartbeats.

My fingers hovered on the reply button. But I couldn't.

Not yet.

Instead, I opened my brother's messages.

VtheMan: *Threads, pick up your goddamn phone.*

VtheMan: *Threads. I'm warning you. You're not happy. I sense it. I'm worried shitless and Tex is being a secretive arsehole. Call me immediately, sister. Or I'll make your life a living hell.*

VtheMan: *Please, Nila. Talk to me. Put me out of my misery. I miss you. Love you so fucking much.*

My teary gasp in the darkness pricked a few hounds' ears. I'd wanted so much to reply. But I didn't dare. I didn't trust myself not to beg him to get me out of this. I was there of my own free will to *protect* him. I wouldn't be protecting him if I was weak.

I wanted hard facts on why the Hawks' could do this. And I wouldn't stop until I knew everything.

Closing my messages, I opened up a picture of Vaughn and me that'd been taken right before the doors opened to the show last night. The tiny bit of strength I had left deserted me and I let go of my tight control.

I sobbed.

My heart expunged its grief through my eyes, drenching my cheeks, blurring the last photo I had of my brother . I cried until dehydration throbbed my head and my neck was sticky with salt.

A low battery reminder beeped. It was the hardest thing I'd done to shut down the picture of V and turn it off.

More tears trickled and a hound raised his head, looking at me with wise understanding. He inched forward on his belly, crossing the hay until his claws tugged at my blanket.

His canine concern produced another torrent, but I opened my arms, and with a wagging tail, he fitted himself around me like a living shield. His doggy heart thudded against mine as I hugged his silky coat.

I went from the Darling of Milan with needle pricks on her fingers to huddled on the floor with only hunting dogs for company.

A soppy tongue had licked my cheek, stealing the endless stream. And that was when it happened. The change I'd told Kite about. The ending. The beginning. The freedom of just letting go.

All my life, I'd been stressed with making a name for myself, building my career, loving my brother, being a worthy daughter. Bills. Deadlines. Reputations. *Expectations.* It all balanced precariously on my shoulders, moulding me into a quiet workaholic.

But at four a.m., in the kennels of the man who meant to kill me, I let it all go.

I said goodbye to control. I waved farewell to everything that made me live, but had also suffocated me, too. I didn't have photo shoots to worry about anymore. I didn't have concerns on what to wear, where to be, how to act.

All of that had been stolen. And there was no point crying or fighting against it.

The moment I embraced the freedom of nothing, I stopped crying. My headache left, and I drifted to sleep wrapped in the four legs of my new best friend.

Squirrel nudged my hand, bringing me back to the present and the waiting message from Kite. The past struggled to let me go, but I blinked, dispelling my forlornness.

"He wants to know where I am. What should I tell him?" I asked my entourage of hounds.

Foxhounds to be exact. Their black, tan, and white coats became visible as the sun rose, glinting off their glossy fur. Their silky ears slapped their pretty heads as they lopped around the enclosure, waking up as the sun grew brighter.

They didn't give me an answer.

Needle&Thread: *Where I am right now doesn't matter because I'm in a fantasy with you. I'm in your bed. Naked.*

It was much better than the truth. I focused on the huge roller door. I'd checked last night to see if there was a way out, but of course, there wasn't.

Kite007: *You took a while to reply. Did you pleasure yourself?*

Throwing myself back into Kite's sexual world, I replied.

Needle&Thread: *I'm coming now. Both hands are between my legs, feeling how wet I am. I'm crying out your name over and over. The neighbours might hear me I'm so loud.*

"Don't tell him I released my tension by crying myself to sleep with you in my arms." Rubbing the head of Squirrel, I smiled. "And don't tell him I've never had an orgasm."

The dog cocked his head, an expression of confusion on his face.

Kite007: *I like it when you talk dirty. Keep going. I have my cock in my hand and want you to make me come.*

My heart sped up. Reclining against the hay bale, I bit my lip. I'd never made anyone come. The drunken night of losing my virginity didn't count because we were both so intoxicated it was a miracle he found the right place to stick it in. After a few half-hearted thrusts, he'd rolled off me to throw up, and I'd pulled up my knickers. I'd been silently horrified at the blood on the sheets.

The copious amounts of alcohol had stolen any pain I might've felt when he penetrated me. It'd also stolen the rush of entering womanhood, swapping it with age-old regret.

The night definitely hadn't been a success. Or the next day. Because no matter how hard V tried to hide my hangover from Tex, he couldn't prevent me from vomiting on my dad's shoes when he plucked me from my bed and took me to the doctor.

I groaned in remembered embarrassment. "He found out, you know." I scratched Squirrel behind his large ear. "The doctor told him I'd been taken advantage of. We'd used protection but it didn't stop the endless STI tests or pregnancy exams." Another hound slinked closer, plopping next to me, looking for a scratch. "That was the last time I was alone with a man other than my dad or brother. Sad isn't it?"

The dog panted, looking as if I'd told the world's best joke.

Maybe Tex prevented you from dating, so when they came for you it was only his *heart you broke—not a husband or children.*

The sudden thought stole my vision with horror.

Was the overprotectiveness to shield *others*? Had he kept me locked up like some princess in a tower, all to stop me being my mother?

He'd fallen in love with my mother.

They'd had children young.

They'd come for her.

I rubbed my chest, unable to stop the epiphany shedding my father in a new light. Was it selfish of him to protect me from living, knowing I was destined an early grave? Or merely a tragedy that he prevented others enduring heartbreak by loving me.

Vaughn.

He would sense the moment my life was snuffed out. We were linked more than spiritually—but soul-glued and breath-bound. I'd known when he broke his collarbone from kayaking. He'd known when I'd dropped my heavy Singer sewing machine onto my foot.

Linked.

Don't think about it. It hurt too damn much. Tears pricked my eyes but I blinked them back, trying to remain in my false bubble of sexting. This was all I had. I could flirt with Kite with complete safety, knowing I would never be able to break his heart when the time came.

In a way, his fastidious request for distance protected him. And for that, I was oddly grateful.

I smiled softly at Squirrel. "If a drunken whoopsy daisy was my only attempt at making a man come, how the hell am I supposed to do it via a faceless message?"

Be someone you're not. Pretend.

"Fine."

Swiping at the dirty mixture of hay, dog hair, and dust from the blanket Jethro had given me, I prepared to embrace my inner sex-kitten.

Needle&Thread: *Imagine your hand is my hand. I'm holding you firm, tight. I'm kneeling at your feet while you sit on a large chair. A throne. Your hand wraps in my hair, pulling me forward. I obey because I know what you're asking me to do. Your eyes don't ask, they tell, and I lower my head into your lap. You're big. Smooth. Begging for my mouth.*

My breath came faster; my mind playing out the fantasy in crystal detail. The warmth I'd been looking for spread from my core like a tentative sunrise.

Kite007: *Fuck me, woman. Why haven't you been talking to me like that all along? What was with the shy bullshit? Keep going. I'm so damn hard. I want your mouth so fucking much.*

My skin broke out in goosebumps. The power. The *approval*. Kite was a wanker, an arsehole, and a complete shallow prick, but he approved of me. He *wanted* me.

Needle&Thread: *You're holding your cock while I lick you once at the very tip. You want me to swallow you, but you don't force me. Because you know I'm going to swallow every drop.*

Kite007: *Did you taste it?*

I frowned.

Needle&Thread: *Taste what?*

Kite007: *My precum. Fuck, I'm so close. I'm in your mouth. I'm fucking your lips. I'm holding your hair as I drive so deep down your throat. What do I taste like to you?*

Needle&Thread: *You taste…*

"Hell, I don't know." Looking at the cluster of dogs, all watching me as if they knew what I was up to, I swiped a hand over my face. "What the hell does a man taste like?"

Needle&Thread: *You taste of expensive liquor, making me drunk as you come. Spilling over my lips, dripping down my chin. You don't want me wasting a drop, so you capture the liquid on your thumb and push it back into my mouth.*

The instant I sent it, a chill darted in my blood.

Thumb. Mouths. Sucking.

Him.

My taste buds brought back the crisp taste of Jethro. His unyielding hold on my chin as I licked his finger. He hadn't really had a taste. Just the cold precision of stone. But having him dominate had given me the permission to feel a flutter in my core, to not be embarrassed of wanting more. Of becoming wet.

Kite007: *Fuck me. I haven't come like that in a while. It's all over me—splashed up my chest, sticking to me like glue. I like you like this, naughty nun. You're more...relaxed.*

My voice was soft. "That's what happens when your life is no longer your own and there's nothing you can do to control your future."

Squirrel yipped in agreement.

"That's also what you do to survive. You become different. You change."

As much as I hated the Hawks, they'd given me something I'd been searching for all my life.

My little kitten claws were growing, prickling. Still too new to scratch with—but there.

My battery flashed again and I knew this would be the last time I'd have the luxury of using it until Jethro let me charge.

Ignoring the emptiness inside and the sharp twinge of letting Kite use me, I sent my last message.

Needle&Thread: *I'm glad. I'm licking you clean. I'm drunk on everything you've given me. I'll be here for you when you next need a release, but please...don't call me naughty nun anymore. Call me Needle.*

Jethro came for me at eleven a.m.

The horses across the yard were gone—to do what, I had no clue. I'd spent an hour or so listening to the grooms prepare them and the comforting *clack* of their metal shoes disappearing into the distance on cobblestones.

I pictured myself commandeering one and galloping away. Not that I knew how to ride. I'd never had time. Sewing had been my one obsession.

Squirrel and his gang of hounds had left not long after I finished messaging Kite. A piercing whistle summoned and they'd charged from the kennel through a small dog-size exit down the back. I'd tried to follow—to get free—but it only opened if a coded collar was in range. A password programmed to every dog allowing them access.

So, I'd spent the remainder of my morning alone. Alone with thoughts I flatly ignored.

It was odd to sit and do nothing. I had nowhere to rush off to. No emails to reply to. No to-do list to attack. I was in limbo, just waiting for the man I loathed to appear.

My stomach was a ball of knots wanting him to get it over with, whilst my jangled heart wanted him to stay away forever. I'd never felt so jumbled inside.

Hunger pangs growled for food—the empty ache only grew worse.

Jethro swung open the top partition of the barn door, leaving the bottom closed. Resting his arms on the top, he nodded. "Ms. Weaver."

The sun took the liberty of bouncing into the gloomy kennel, silhouetting Jethro. His face remained in shadow but his thick hair was wet and messy from a shower.

He'd shed his charcoal suit for a more casual grey shirt, the diamond pin twinkling in his lapel. I'd grown to recognize it as his signature piece, linking him to whatever organisation his father ran.

Is it a gang? Did they rob and cheat and kill?

It wasn't my issue. I didn't care. I was the innocent party—their hostage.

I didn't return his greeting, deciding to stay bundled in my blanket and glower.

Jethro sniffed impatiently, removing his arms from the door. He unlocked the bottom partition, swinging it wide.

More sunshine entered, illuminating the bottom half of his wardrobe. Dark jeans. Well-fitted jeans. Jeans that made him seem young and approachable and *normal*.

My hands balled. *Don't buy into the projection.* There was nothing normal about this man. Nothing sane or kind. I learned that last night—many times over. There would be no more begging from me. No more pleading. It fell on deaf ears, and I was done.

Jethro snapped his fingers as if expecting me to heel. "Get up. It's time to begin." Taking a threatening step into the kennel, he pursed his lips. "Shit, what did you do in your sleep? Roll around like the dogs?"

I kept my lips pressed together, watching him in the silence he so seemed to enjoy. When I didn't move, his face twisted, taking in my hay-riddled hair and dirt-covered blanket. "I won't tell you again. Get. Up."

I shrugged. It was liberating to no longer care. To no longer be captive by the need to obey and jump to attention for fear of retribution. I meant what I said to Kite. Everything inside me was gone. Locked down, bunkered inside, ready to weather whatever war was coming.

Standing slowly, I placed my dead phone into my jacket pocket. Letting the blanket fall off my hips, I brushed lingering lint off my clothes.

Jethro snapped his fingers again, and I moved willingly—coasting to his side exactly as he wanted.

He scowled, his gaze full of suspicion.

I gave him an empty smile. I'd found salvation in not caring. It didn't mean I had to pretend to like him. He wouldn't know that by trying to break me last night, he only gave me a new avenue of strength.

I'm ready.

For whatever he threw at me.

I'll survive.

Until I no longer needed to try.

Running my hands through my hair, I quickly gave up with the tangles and focused on pinching some colour into my cheeks instead.

"You think that will save you? Looking presentable?" His voice was blizzard and snow.

I didn't say a word.

Jethro gritted his jaw. His hands curled beside his spread

legs.

My muscles braced for punishment. The air shimmered with violence.

Jethro's hand suddenly shot out, capturing my throat. Without a sound, he spun me around and marched me backward out of the kennel. The sun kissed my skin, fanning the warmth I'd tried so hard to keep hold of from talking to Kite. I embraced it, hugging it close, so Jethro's ice didn't slice me into pieces.

His fingers tightened around my neck, but I refused to claw at his hold. *I repay in kind.* Whatever I did to him in self-defence, I'd get back ten times worse. But none of that mattered now, because I knew how to survive.

By being above them. By being untouchable on the inside, even while they broke me on the outside.

"You think you've got it all figured out, don't you?" His arm hoisted me onto the tips of my toes. Breathing was difficult, not fighting was impossible, but I permitted it. All I did was stare silently into his golden eyes.

"I understand what you're doing." He smiled. "But mark my words. You won't win." Shaking me, he unwound his fingers, then smoothed the front of his jeans. The sun gleamed on the gold buckle of his belt.

My stomach clenched, but I held my ground. "Mark *my* words. I will win. Because I am right and you are wrong."

Jethro seethed, silence thick between us.

"You're so high and mighty, aren't you, Ms. Weaver? So sure you're the one in the right. What if I told you, your ancestors were scum? What if I showed you proof of their corruptibility and eagerness to hurt others in their chase for wealth?"

Lies. All lies.

My family tree was impeccable. I came from honest and good and hardworking stock. Didn't I?

I ignored my rushing heartbeat.

Jethro stepped closer, crowding me. "The things your

family did to mine sicken me. So continue on your quest believing you're pure, because in a few hours you'll know the truth. In a few hours, you'll realise we aren't the bad guys—it's you."

My throat closed up. I didn't think he could say anything to crumble my fortress so soon, but every word was a carefully planted spade, digging at my foundation until I stood on crumbling ground.

My eyes danced over his, trying to decipher the truth.

Were my bloodlines tarnished with crimes I didn't know about? My father hadn't exactly been forthcoming with our history, apart from telling us our family had always been involved in weaving and textiles. It was how we were granted the last name Weaver. Just like the Bakers, and the Butlers, and every other trade that dictated their last names.

Jethro chuckled. "Don't believe me?" His hands landed on my shoulders, pushing me backward. I stumbled, wincing as my spine collided with the bricked wall of the kennel.

"Don't believe your forefathers were sentenced to death by hanging for what they did to mine?" His gaze latched onto my mouth. "Don't believe you're alive because the Hawks granted them mercy in return for a few signatures on a few debts?"

His voice dropped, sending a constellation of warning over my skin. "Don't believe I'm fully within my right to do whatever I damn well please to you?"

His touch seared through my jacket and maxi dress, sending unwanted intensity down my arms.

Do I believe it? Could I believe it? That everything I understood of this situation was reversed?

Mind games. Illusions. All designed to trip me up.

Shaking my head, I snapped, "No. I don't believe it." My blood pressure exploded, thundering in my ears. His focus was absolute, and it burned, oh how it burned. "Nothing you say will make you the victim in this situation. Nothing you show me will make this permissible. You think I believe a ludicrous debt that you say is over six hundred years old. Wake up! Nothing like that would hold up in a court of law these days. I don't care that you've staged my disappearance, or following my family with a loaded pistol. I don't believe any of this, and I certainly don't believe you have anything law abiding on your side."

Jethro scowled, but I continued my tyrant.

"All I believe is you're a bunch of sick and twisted men who made up some bullshit excuse to make themselves feel justified while tearing other's lives apart. Show me where you have the right to own me. No one has that right. No one!"

He chuckled, gold eyes growing dark. His body language switched from stand-offish to oozing with sexual innuendo. It was like watching a glacier melt, shedding winter for volcanic heat.

"I like it when you're feisty. Your whole perception of the world is warped. You live in a fairytale, princess, and I'm about to destroy it."

His shoulders softened, lips parting; his gaze caressed my face to land on my mouth. "You think we don't have men in high places? Men who make what we say absolute law? You think we got to the level of standing in society or the obscene amount of wealth we have by not using the very same law you think will protect you for our gain?"

His voice whispered over me, threading with his heady scent of woods and leather. "So stupid, Ms. Weaver. We own more than your family. We own everything and everyone. Our word is unbreakable. And we have proof."

He leaned in; the violence he emitted switched to dangerous lust, buffeting me harder against the wall. His eyes were rivers of fire, annihilating my argument, dragging me under his spell. "You think I can't make you do what I want?"

I sucked in a breath.

He'd never looked at me like that. Never given any hint he might find anything about me exciting. He treated me like a leper. He looked at me as if I were a different species—a species not evolved enough to warrant his sexual attention.

But that'd changed.

His interest trapped me, consuming me better than threats and tightly restrained anger. This was unexplored territory. Lust and attraction and flirting were terrifying, because I was the novice and he was the expert.

I couldn't fight against something that made me *feel*.

Jethro's nostrils flared, fingers twitching on my shoulders. His voice lowered to a husky whisper—a whisper best suited for seduction. "You think you deserve a life built on other's blood? You think you're worthy?" The rhythm and volume turned the horrible questions into a poem rather than curse.

Don't fall for it. Don't let him win.

He was already winning. He spun a tale of a lethal, unstoppable force. His family's legacy somehow granted him police approval, government blind-eyes, and the right over life and death.

Who *gave* him that right?

I still couldn't believe it. But it didn't stop my legs shifting, pressing together, trying to alleviate the strange ache building with every moment.

Our fighting coaxed my unseen claws to grow a little more. My temper made my legs firmer; my vision clearer. My body unknowingly found a cure from dreaded vertigo, all while embracing anger and rage.

Jethro noticed my tension, stroking my shoulders as if I were a skittish prey. "We're simple creatures, Ms. Weaver. I know what's happening to you." He smiled gently, his gold eyes attempting to look soft, but unable to hide the steel beneath. "Your skin is hot. You're breathing faster."

He ducked his head, murmuring, "You like this. You like being pushed past your limits."

I shook my head. "You're wrong. There's nothing about you that I like."

He sighed, his gaze whispering over my mouth. "Lying won't work. I know you're growing wet for me, wanting me."

His touch morphed from menacing to lightning, sending a rain of sparks through my blood. "Want to know how I know? Because I taste it in the air. I smell it all around you. I *feel* it."

My lips parted. My chest rose and fell, increasing faster and faster. I couldn't look away; I couldn't push him away. I couldn't do anything but revel in the intoxicating, melting, glowing, sparking need building rapidly in my core.

Closing my eyes, I swallowed hard, trying so hard to dispel the sick and twisted desire he conjured. "I'm—I'm not."

He ran his thumbs over my shoulders, following my collarbone with infinite softness. "You're not?" he breathed. "You're not feeling the rush of lust or the knowledge you'd throw all your rules away for just…one…little…taste?" His lips came so close to mine, pulling away in the ultimate tease.

Yes. No. I don't know.

I'd lost control of my body, hurtling straight for a cataclysm where everything was hot and sharp and intense.

I didn't have an answer. I didn't know what he wanted.

He's fucking with your mind. That's all he's doing.

His thumbs stroked higher, smoothing away the bruises he'd caused on my neck. "Tell me you're not wet for me. Say it."

I shook my head, willing the words to come. "I'm not. I'm…"

"What?" Jethro murmured.

The ache grew stronger, sending a rush of dampness against my knickers. My body didn't care this was a monster. My body didn't care about the future. All it cared about was curbing the intolerable need.

Opening my heavy eyes, I said, "I'm not wet. Not for you."

My hands balled, fighting against the thick intoxication. I couldn't let him steal the warmth from Kite. He'd already turned the small flame into an out of control inferno, cindering my morals, turning my hatred to ash. I couldn't fall into his web—he'd eat me alive.

But, one kiss…would it be so wrong?

To take something from him when he'd already taken so much from me?

I swayed closer, unconsciously seeking everything he dangled before me. I wasn't equipped to play these games. I was naïve and woefully unprepared for combat where lust was used as the weapon.

"You're a little liar, Ms. Weaver." He dropped one hand from my shoulders, tracing my contours until he captured my hip, the other skated upward, cupping my cheek. Every millimetre he travelled sent sparks along my skin unlike anything I'd ever felt before.

His tongue appeared, licking his lips. "You want this." His knee nudged against mine, forcing my legs to spread. "You want something you know you shouldn't." With seamless authority, he pressed against me, tilting his hips into mine.

I shivered. Hating him. Lusting for him. Hating myself. Loving the forbidden rush.

The reasons for our fight flew away on soundless wings, leaving me with no argument against the swelling swollen ache.

"All that separates my cock from your pussy is a few fragile pieces of clothing." He drove upward, grinding himself punishingly. "You won't stop me." There was no space, no secrets—our bodies glued together.

My mind went blank with sheer-numbing pleasure. I felt every ridge and contour of him. From the pressure of his shoe against mine to the hot heat in his jeans growing larger every second.

You know what he intends to do. Stop this, I screamed at my betraying body. But it replied in force with a clenching ripple, turning my legs to jelly.

I held my breath. His hard body was as unmovable as the wall I stood trapped against. His ripped stomach pressed against mine.

I wasn't cushy or curvy. I had no feminine attributes—I'd exercised away any hope at softness.

But it only amplified the intensity.

There was nothing to cushion the firmness of bones and sinew and craving flesh. It was visceral. All consuming.

"Tell me again you're not wet for me." His hooded eyes imprisoned mine. "Tell me another lie."

I tried to look away, but he thrust again, enticing another ripple of pleasure. I hadn't planned on being the innocent girl. The stuck-up princess who never self-pleasured or enjoyed men. I hated that I came across priggish, uptight, and repressed. Those traits were a hazard of my upbringing, and I desperately wanted to turn them into weapons.

I wanted to use them as effortlessly as Jethro wielded his wintery charisma.

My body knew what it wanted. It wanted a release. It wanted to satiate and be sated. And it didn't give a flying arse who granted the freedom of the mysterious orgasm. I knew who Jethro was—I knew this was all a game to him. But why couldn't two people play? Why did I have to justify his touch as bad when it was so amazingly *good*?

Death was coming. Shouldn't I try to *live* before I died?

For once in my life.

Be true and honest and raw.

Why can't I use him? Just once be the bad girl and use the monster. Win by not fighting. Be stronger by giving in.

My pussy grew bolder, taking my unvoiced permission and growing wet, greedy, eager to experience the cock pressed firmly against me.

I…can't.

You can.

I…won't.

You will.

Jethro ducked, nipping my jaw with sharp teeth.

I unlocked my chastity belt, and melted into him. I arched my back, deliberately pressing my breasts against his chest.

His seduction lost the calculating edge, his breath went from calm to uneven.

Something new broke free inside. Some level of embarrassment of sex—the unapproved thoughts of being used—disappeared. I was a business woman. A daughter. A sister. The fantasies inside weren't the thoughts of a puritan.

Deep inside, where I never let myself go, a sexual deviant lurked. A woman who was bold and angry. A woman beyond ready to admit she'd hidden so much of herself—even from herself.

Jethro's hand moved to grab the back of my neck. His hips pulsed; his heart thudded hard, vibrating our tightly pressed forms.

I shivered in his hold, giving in completely to the clench between my legs.

"Answer me. Tell me the truth." His mint-fresh breath fluttered my eyelashes as he hovered possessively over my lips. Only a tiny space between a tease and a kiss. Only a fraction between right and wrong.

Do it. Accept it.

He paused, murmuring into my mouth, "Tell me a secret. A dirty, dark secret. Admit you want me. Admit you want your mortal enemy."

I admit it.

"I won't." My heartbeat switched from thumping to humming; my skin prickled with heat.

I hated him. I wanted to kill him before he killed me. But I couldn't ignore the overwhelming attraction he'd created. And it wasn't just me affected. His breathing turned ragged; his fingers dug deeper with need. Every pulse of his hips drew a quickening in my core. I couldn't control it. I didn't *want* to control it. I was done controlling my life.

I'm free.

The longer we stood, the further we blurred the lines between debtor and debtee. Weaver and Hawk. In that tiny moment, we were each other's answer to freedom. A mind-blistering coupling that would surely ruin me for life. But at least I would've *lived*.

I looked deep into Jethro's burning eyes, transmitting everything I suffered. *I hate you for making me acknowledge this part of myself.*

His face tightened; his body slammed harder against mine. Whispering his lips over my cheek, bringing them low, lower, lower, the tip of his tongue tasted the corner of my mouth.

My world disintegrated with an ecliptic *bang*.

I trembled, eyes snapping closed on their own accord.

His hand on my hip shot downward, disappearing between our bodies.

I gasped, jolting in his hold as his fingers scrunched up my dress, shoving it out of the way as if it were nothing. My gasp turned to a ragged moan as he cupped me bold and strong. My gaze flew wide, locking onto his.

Never had something felt so good. So bad. So intensely delicious.

His gold eyes turned to a burnt sunset, filling with fire as he fingered my knickers. "Do you think you're so perfect you wouldn't scream my name? Do you think you'd be able to say no if I dragged you into the kennel and fucked you?" His fingers bit into my pussy, hot and punishing. "Because I want to. Fuck, how I want to. I want your screams. I want you begging."

I lost myself completely, throwing myself into this new creation. The one who had the power to do this and still retain her heart. The one who would give Jethro her body because *she* wanted it. Not him.

His fingers scattered my thoughts, probing against the thin satin of my underwear. His touch was electrifying. I wanted more. I wanted everything.

I stepped off the cliff. "No. I'm not so perfect. And yes, I would scream." Clawing at his shoulders, I forced myself deeper onto his hand. "You think I'm immune? You think I'm dry and repulsed by you?" Dragging him closer, I murmured, "You couldn't be more wrong."

Jethro's nostrils flared. His fingers twitched as he

narrowed his eyes. "You think you can confuse me?"

I pressed a finger against his mouth. "Shut up."

His eyes popped wide; he growled low in his chest. His lips pulled back, revealing sharp teeth.

I didn't remove my finger. *I* was in charge. *I* was the one taking. "My heart hates you, but my body….I'm drenched. I'm begging. So stop your endless questions. Stop taunting me and deliver."

Kite flew into my mind, then was gone. I'd surpassed awkward sexting, embracing physical coyness.

The world paused for a millisecond.

Jethro sucked in a shocked breath. Then his hand left my pussy, tore the small stitches holding my knickers in place, and drove one finger so damn deep inside me, I did what I said I would.

I screamed.

My head fell back, smashing against the wall. My heart exploded into a mess of passion and rage.

Oh, God. Oh, *God*.

My mouth sucked in air, but it didn't stop the swirling, blinding need stealing my remaining sanity, giving me completely and utterly to Jethro. I cried inside. I wailed inside. I wished I could be different. Someone not so deprived of her animalistic needs. Someone who could scream and call for help. Not someone who tilted their hips and moaned at the curses spilling from Jethro's lips. Not someone who gripped the man who tore her from her world and opened her legs wider.

But then Jethro touched a spot that made my muscles lock and a need so violent to seize. I grabbed his wrist, forcing him to take me harder. My tears turned to joy, writhing on Jethro's hand.

"Fuck. Me." His voice was sex-gruffed and so low it echoed over cobblestones. "Who the hell are you?" His finger worked me, pulsating deep inside.

I opened my legs as wide as I could. I gave up on everything, embracing the simplicity of being a sexually starved creature.

This wasn't making love. This wasn't even fucking. This was war. And hell it felt good.

Digging my fingernails into his shoulders, I jerked him closer. "Harder."

Jethro groaned, and in a twist of fate—obeyed. His finger drove so deep his knuckles nudged against my swollen flesh. His thumb swirled around my clit, smearing wetness, taking me to ever new heights.

I turned to stone before detonating into tiny pieces. Every inch of my thoughts, emotions, and reactions were stolen by his mind-blowing touch. I hadn't felt anything like it.

Guilt tried to claim me, reminding me this was the man who ruined my life. But lust quickly devoured the guilt, turning it to raging passion.

"You're so fucking tight," he growled, thrusting his finger harder.

I felt as if I'd not been living. As if my world was dark and Jethro was the sun bringing me nutrition I never knew I needed.

A painful pressure burned as he tried to fit two fingers inside me.

I flinched, rocking my hips away. "Stop—"

He paused, then removed the second digit, driving a single finger deep, dragging me back to willing. "You're a virgin. The rumours were true."

I shook my head. "No."

"No?" He grabbed my chin, holding me firm, driving his finger harder. I cried out, letting my head loll on my useless neck with bliss. "How are you this tight and not a virgin?"

"Once. I only—" I stopped, consumed with every pulse of Jethro's finger. "I'm—"

I gave up.

I was completely illiterate.

"If you're not a virgin, prove it." His fingers tightened around my chin. "Pull out my cock."

My mind blanked out. I hung onto the precipice of my good girl ways before throwing myself head first into a woman who would do anything to feel alive.

"Pull out my cock, Ms. Weaver." He thrust against me, battering me with the hardness in his jeans.

My eyes flared wide. My stomach hollowed out at the same time it swooped upright as he thrust his finger.

"Goddammit," he growled. "Do it. I'm not going to come in my jeans like an idiot."

Would he fuck me? If I took out his cock, would he take me?

Sex? With him?

I...

I couldn't have sex with him. This cold-hearted monster. But my raging heart and bubbling blood said *yes*. God, yes.

Shutting off my thoughts, I dropped my hands from his shoulders and fumbled with the buckle of his belt.

The hardness of his erection burned my fingertips. Jethro didn't help my concentration, driving his touch deeper. "Hurry up. I need your sweet fingers jerking me off. Goddammit, I don't know—" His voice cut off as I undid his button and zipper.

I gasped as his cock sprang out, escaping the top of his grey boxer-briefs. He shuddered, groaning in relief. The tip glistened with wetness, slightly red, slightly swollen.

My eyes grew wide, fear chasing away the lust in my veins. I looked up, swallowing hard. "You're...I can't—"

He scowled. "Too late to back out now, woman." Grabbing my hand, he placed it roughly around his thick, hard *massive* cock. I had no experience to go on, but he would *never* fit inside me. He wouldn't fit inside any woman.

"Shut up and stroke me."

I opened my mouth, unable to form words. "It can't—there's no way—"

In a lightning fast move, he jerked his finger from my core, smearing my dampness on my cheek as he pinched me hard. "You're out of excuses, Ms. Weaver. You were the one who started this. You're the one who rode my finger as if you'd never come before." His voice dropped to a dark whisper. "So shut up, wrap those little fingers around my cock and stroke me; otherwise, I swear to God I'll throw you on your hands and knees and fuck your tight little cunt right here."

My heart lurched. There wouldn't be anything erotic about that. It would hurt. He would split me in two.

Biting my lip, I cupped the exposed head, spreading the sticky residue at the top down his hot shaft. Locking eyes with Jethro, I pushed my hand into his boxers, following his long, long length.

His eyes snapped closed as my timid fingers latched round him. "Fuuuuck," he groaned. His forehead smashed against mine, hips pulsating into my hand. "Stop taunting me. Harder, goddammit."

That was asking for the impossible. I couldn't get my fingers to connect around his girth. My grip was useless around the throbbing heat—the only hot part of him. Holding my breath, I wrapped my hold as hard as I could.

Jethro grunted. "Squeeze it. Stop being a fucking tease. Was I teasing you?" His hand suddenly disappeared up my dress again, his middle finger thrusting so hard and quick inside me, he sent a galaxy of stars exploding behind my eyes.

Then he glided upward, smearing the wetness around my clit. My legs tried to scissor closed; all my attention shot between my legs.

I went rigid. Having him touch me was amazing. Having him rub that small bundle of nerves was *incredible*.

"Return the favour, Ms. Weaver. Make me come. Right here. Right now. And I'll drive you so wild, you'll beg and never want anyone else."

Coming. The blissful end of sex. Was that what the sharp sensation was? Growing tighter and tighter in my core? If it was, I wanted to come.

Badly.

Winding my fingers as tight as possible around his girth, I squeezed until a jagged pain erupted down my palm. I didn't have the strength. I didn't know what to do. Did I just squeeze and let him thrust into my hand? What else was expected?

With a low growl, Jethro stopped stroking my clit. He turned to granite. "*That's* your idea of making me come?"

I swallowed, jerking my hand away. The thrill of being touched and touching faded, rapidly replaced with despair. "I'm—yes…uh."

"For fuck's sake." Rolling his eyes, he removed his hand from between my legs and stepped back. With a grunt, he yanked his trousers back into place, but not before I caught a glimpse of just how huge his cock was. It was flawlessly straight, veiny, silky, so proud and rigid—just like its owner.

It terrified me.

"Fuck, what was I thinking? You're useless. Completely useless." Buckling his belt, he ran his hands through his hair, smearing the lingering wetness from me through his silvering strands. "*Huge* disappointment, Ms. Weaver." His cold glare sent a snowstorm wiping away the bonfire in my belly. "I'm done playing games, so cut the bullshit. Time to begin the day." His voice gave no room for interpretation. A cold draft shot down my back.

My brief reprieve from debts and horrible Hawks was over. I'd been shown something I desperately wanted, but was denied it because I failed to please him.

"You could teach me…show me how…" I couldn't make eye contact with him. Mortification painted my cheeks for both admitting I was clueless and asking a monster to coach me.

Jethro laughed. "You think that will save you from what's coming? Was that your little plan? To make me fuck you in the hopes I might *feel* something for you?" He shook his head. "I'm not teaching you anything—especially how to jerk me off. As you told me once—Google that shit—but it won't do you any good, because next time…I won't need your hand to come."

My breath caught in my throat.

My heart hung heavy and I shivered. The sun crept behind a cloud, leaving us in haunting shadows.

Jethro stood glaring, the outline of his erection visible in his jeans. But there was no hint of the lust he'd suffered, or the passion that blazed between us only seconds before. His unfeeling eyes burned a hole straight into my soul, condemning me for my past treasons and present failures. The longer he stared, the more he undermined my carefully built fortress.

I couldn't stand the intensity any longer. The humiliation of standing there unwanted, slightly used, and entirely frustrated. With shaking hands, I smoothed down my dress and pushed away from the wall. Without a word, I flicked my hair over my shoulder and skirted around him. With confident steps, I left him behind, heading toward the manor.

He'll chase. He'll hunt.

I expected to land on my face from a carefully planned strike. I waited for vertigo to steal my quiet assurance and spiral me to the ground. But nothing happened.

Jethro didn't pounce, and I didn't fall.

I was steady for the first time in my life.

My world continued even though I'd been thrown off my axis and into a brand new realm. A realm where sex beckoned like the Holy Grail and my self-hatred magnified a thousand fold.

My empty stomach threatened to steal the remaining strength in my limbs, but I kept going, ignoring my body's protests, walking like a good little animal to the slaughter.

I didn't think I was about to enjoy my penance of being a Weaver.

Balling my hands, I made a promise. A promise I hoped would grant me strength for the coming days.

They can't touch me. I'm not Nila or Threads. I'm done being weak.

My heart swelled as I crested the hill, staring at Hawksridge Hall in all its glory. I shed my kitten baby-fur and embraced a new pelt. One that filled me with fight. One that embraced the elongating claws I'd begun to grow.

I was no longer protected by tigers but forced to become one.

I'm Needle, and I will survive.

Jethro

CONTROL.

I loved it.

I wielded it.

I *owned* it.

But that little Weaver broke my control, turning me into nothing more than a sex-driven idiot. She'd made me throw my decorum, calmness, and carefully laid plans out the goddamn window.

Her timid fingers. Her fluttering breaths. They'd been more of a turn on than the most experienced of lovers. She was so fucking pure she choked on a halo.

And to ask me to *teach* her? Granting me power by evolving this virginal creature into anything I damn well wanted?

It was temptation.

It was not fucking permitted.

She was mine to take from. Mine to share.

I refused to train her, because in the end *I* would be the one delivering the killing blow. She wouldn't succeed in dragging me into whatever game she played.

I breathed hard, even now struggling to find my beloved coldness. I needed an icy shower. *I need to teach her a fucking lesson—that's what I need.*

A knock snapped my head up. I spun in place, trading the view of the front gardens to glare at my father. The man who'd taught me how to be the master of my emotions. How to rein in the uncouth part of ourselves and be ruthless with silence. He'd taught me the most—beaten me the most—and I was his favourite.

Thank God there were no cameras by the stables—if he saw how far I fell, his disappointment would bring repercussions. Big repercussions.

My father popped his head into the 'Buzzard Room' named for the hand-stencilled wallpaper of hunting buzzards and the mounted carcasses of ducks, swans, and small birds.

It was also the room I'd picked for Nila. This would be her quarters—a room stinking of death and decay.

She'd somehow won the lesson I wanted to teach her at the kennels. She'd managed to make me trade control for the promise of sex. It had worked.

It. Would. Not. Work. Again.

I pitied her really. She'd shown me so much in that brief moment. She was hungry. She was hidden. And she was so damn vulnerable it made me smile to think of her illusions. She thought she could outsmart us.

Us?

Diamond merchants, biker royalty, and proven masters of the Weaver's fate.

Stupid, *stupid* girl.

I nodded at my father. "Cut."

His grey goatee bristled. "Bring her into the dining room when she's ready. Everyone's gathered." He puffed on a giant cigar, wearing a tweed waistcoat and trousers complete with a leather jacket from the Black Diamonds. He looked an enigma of motorcycle world and English aristocracy.

I nodded again.

He left without a goodbye, and I moved to sit on the seventeenth century hand-carved brooding chair. A chair made for men and only men. Complete with ashtray, newspaper stand, and heavy, dark brocade designed with our family crest.

Ten minutes later, the door to the ensuite bathroom opened, revealing a freshly showered Nila. Her long black hair draped like ink on her naked shoulders. She looked younger, innocent without the heavy makeup smeared from last night. Her eyes were bigger, like black unhappy pools whilst her skin glowed a natural dusky tan.

I'd seen her in magazines. I'd run a fingertip over her snapshot in the fashion columns, but never found her attractive. She didn't have breasts. She always stood like a fading shadow next to her brother and looked too prim and stuck up.

She was nothing to me.

Then why did I almost come while fingering her?

My mouth watered, remembering the wildness lurking beneath that up-tight-virgin bluff.

I swallowed, battling the blood rushing to my dick. The way she rode my hand—fuck.

Then I laughed. Out loud.

Waving at her tiny hands clutching the towel, I said, "I see your fingers are capable of holding something." My head cocked. "Do I need to remind you what a disappointment earlier was?"

She was nothing to me before, and she would remain nothing to me. And after this afternoon, there would be no way in hell she'd ever let me touch her again.

Which was perfect, because the next time wouldn't be for pleasure. It would be for pain. And permission would take the control away.

She froze, locking her knees. The heavy cloud when she suffered a stupid balance attack swirled in her eyes. Sucking in a breath, she said quietly, "No, you don't. You've told me countless of times. You've made me very aware of what you think of me, and I'm sick of hearing it."

I took my time glancing down her body.

She didn't fidget or blush, which pissed me off. I wanted

her nervous. I wanted her terrified of what was to come.

I stood up slowly, clicking my tongue. "Ah, ah, ah, Ms. Weaver. Don't take that tone with me. You're the failure. *You're* the prisoner. You take what I give you. You do not assume to have any say or authority. That includes listening to everything I deem important to tell you." Ghosting to a stop in front of her, I murmured, "Is that quite understood?"

I flexed my muscles, welcoming back the soothing chillness of control. I hadn't liked stepping outside my confines of civility. Things got messy when silence was disrupted. Things got rushed when tempers rose and curses flowed.

And I couldn't handle that.

Running a fingertip along her damp shoulder, I smiled at her flinch. "Did you do as I asked and wash your filth away?"

Her lips pursed, anger glowing in her eyes. But she swallowed it down, muting the light. "Yes."

"Did you leave your pussy alone? No trying to finish what I started?"

Her head hung a little lower. "Yes."

My finger followed the contour of her shoulder, tracing down her arm. She stood silently, hiding the wild creature from before, depicting quiet sexuality and vulnerability. My mouth watered again, but it wasn't with need to shove her against the wall and drive my dick inside her. No, it was because I'd never made someone with her skin colour bleed. Would her blood be darker? Would it be a rich chocolate like her eyes?

I knew her family tree. I'd studied it in preparation. Her bloodlines weren't pure—there was mixed race in her past. A blend of Spanish and English. Another reason why Hawks were better. We were one hundred percent English stock. Unsullied.

Nila looked into my eyes. Her skin broke out in goosebumps. "Stop whatever you're doing and let me get dressed. Where are my clothes?" She clutched the silver towel harder, hiding everything but her longer than average legs and tiny feet. "I need to charge my phone. I want my suitcase."

I didn't bother caring who'd she'd texted last night to drain her battery. There would be no cavalry coming to her rescue—of that I was completely sure. "You'll receive your belongings if you please us."

"Us?"

Stepping back, I smoothed my shirt, taking my time in delivering the truth. I hoped she'd move away—run even. But she locked her knees again, standing firm on the thick mahogany carpet.

"Yes. Us." Holding out my palm, I waited. "Take my hand."

She hesitated, hoisting her towel higher, her tiny fist jammed against her small breasts.

I looked forward to making her obey, but then the aloofness I'd briefly witnessed in the kennels came over her features—blotting out the fire, turning her into an obedient robot.

Slowly she did as I requested, placing her slightly damp hand in mine.

The moment I had her, I marched across the bedroom floor. She gasped, jerked into motion, her legs darting to keep up. Silently, I wrenched open the door and stalked down the huge corridor, past shields and lances and crossbows, to the end of the bachelor wing where the Black Diamond brotherhood met once a week in a club meeting called the Gemstone.

This afternoon, it wasn't business being discussed. It was Nila.

This was her welcome luncheon.

A tradition unbroken for hundreds of years. An esteemed event that all our brethren knew.

The day they all sample a Weaver.

Slamming my palm against the double doors, I jerked Nila into the room. She wheeled to a stop, her face losing its colour in favour of snowy white. I searched her features for fear. I hunted for terror, but I only witnessed blank resignation.

Turning away from her, I focused on what she couldn't look away from.

Men.

Some smooth faced and young, others bearded and old. But they all had something in common. They belonged to the Diamonds and were our most trusted employees. Flaw, Fracture, and Cushion weren't present. Their task was to watch Vaughn and Archibald Weaver from doing anything…reckless.

Nila struggled, trying to take her hand back. I clamped my fingers around her, not giving an inch. "Don't be rude, Ms. Weaver. Say hello and be courteous. This is, after all, your welcome lunch."

She jolted, shying backward, testing my hold.

My father sat at the end of the extremely long table. The room was huge. Decorated with gold-spun drapery and massive oil paintings of my ancestors, it glittered with crystal chandeliers and silverware.

The paintings were of male Hawks only. The women of my family tree were designated to another room. Still celebrated, but not nearly as important.

Each artwork showed a man of distinguished wealth and intolerable power. I'd studied them in great length this past month, preparing for Nila's arrival. My favourite was Owen Hawk.

I looked just like him.

Snapping his fingers, my father called the small murmurs of masculine voices to attention. Pointing at Nila trembling beside me, he said, "Brothers, this woman will be our guest for the foreseeable future, and in honour of her company, we have something special planned."

The men grinned, reclining in their chairs, ready for the show to begin. The hiss and crackle of the log fire added a cheery background noise as well as welcome heat to the cavernous room.

"Jet, if you would be so kind as to make sure our guest is appropriately attired."

Pleasure.

Tradition had begun.

Dropping Nila's hand, I moved toward the large side table that held crockery, wine glasses, and decanters. The food that'd been prepared by the full kitchen in the other wing of the house waited on the matching sideboard across the room. There were countless dishes, at least seven courses, but no wait staff to present it.

I smiled.

That was where Ms. Weaver came in. Along with...other duties.

Gathering the items that were meant for Nila, I returned to her side. She hadn't moved, but not from obedience. Two large men in leather cuts blocked her way out. The moment I came back, she looked pleadingly into my eyes.

"I can't—Jethro, don't make me." She swallowed. "Not so many. I can't do—"

Snatching her arm, I spun her to the corner of the room, away from hungry onlookers. "You dare say no? Do you *want* this to be over?"

She nodded rapidly. "Yes. More than anything yes."

"Fine. It's over. But you're sentenced to watch your father and brother be slaughtered, along with the decimation of your family's business and assets. It will be obliterated. Gone. Is that what you're willing to pay?"

She squeezed her eyes in horror.

Didn't think so.

I never wanted to be that weak. That driven by compassion. I obeyed my family. I accepted my position. But I would *never* let love dictate my actions.

That wasn't what a Hawk did.

We were untouchable.

Taking the liberty of her lack of vision, I placed the first item on her head. A sexy, frilly maid's cap. It perched on her head, gracing her damp black hair like a sad crown.

Her head dipped, shielding her eyes. Her body convulsed,

trying hard to maintain the blankness she thought would be her salvation.

Tugging her hands, I muttered, "Let go of the towel."

She cowered away.

Growling under my breath, I wrapped an arm around her waist, holding her firm. "Don't make me ask again. You're not new to this game. Let go of the towel."

Her eyes flew wide, fighting my hold. "No!"

Goddammit, she tested me. A headache brewed behind my eyes. I sighed. "Make me ask you one more time. Go on…"

She froze, breathing hard. A battle broke out between us. I should never have let her get away with what she pulled at the stables. She thought I'd softened. She thought I'd be lenient. If anything, she'd proven my errors and I'd go above and beyond to ensure I didn't falter again.

Ever.

She had to learn that the day granted hope and happiness, but I stole it. She had to face that the night hid evil and darkness, but my soul was blacker.

There would be no winning. None.

We didn't speak, but our eyes shouted, wrapping us tight with unsaid tension.

Finally, she lowered her chin in defeat. Her death grip on the fluffy material loosened, allowing it to flutter to the floor.

Ordinarily, I would've rewarded her. A kind word. A gentle gesture. But that was before I learned I couldn't give her any softness. She needed a firm, masterful hand. Otherwise, she'd make my life a living hell until I stole hers.

My eyes latched onto her naked body.

I paused.

Fuck.

Nila Weaver was like the needle she used to make her livelihood. Long, sculptured. Muscle tone so defined, her hips defied her supple skin, almost piercing her. Her breasts were small but high with perfect dark nipples.

My gaze dropped between her legs. The part of her I'd

intimately explored already. I expected an inexperienced girl to not maintain her pussy, but there was only a strip of black hair, hiding and teasing at the same time.

My heartbeat thickened.

And then I noticed the bruises.

Everywhere. On her ribcage, hips, thighs, and arms.

I prodded at a particularly large purple one. "Who did this?"

She crossed her knees, clamping a hand over her breasts.

I swallowed hard, hating that my cock twitched.

Her mouth parted, then understanding flared. "Not who. What." Looking down at herself, she whispered, "The perils of vertigo."

I had no reply to that. She already had a condition that hurt her.

I hated that I understand that…more than she knew.

"Put your arm down." I slapped it away from her breasts. She stiffened, but left it by her side, standing taller than before.

Holding out the tiny excuse of an apron, I placed it over her head. It was black with white lacy trim, low enough to show the tops of her breasts and nipples, short enough to show the trimmed delight between her legs.

Spinning her around, I tied the strings at her neck and lower spine. When she faced me again, she choked, "Why?"

"Why?" I raised an eyebrow.

"Is this all a game to you?"

I smiled. "No game. We're deadly serious. As you should know by now." Leaving her, I returned to the table and collected the final item. The Weaver heirloom.

Prowling back to her, I held up the collar.

Her eyes popped wide. She gawked at the solid encrusted diamond collar made from our very own imports. Two hundred carats, valued at over three million pounds—it'd been in my family since the first debt had been claimed.

"Do you know what this is?" I dangled it in front of her face.

She clamped her lips, eyes deathly cold.

I didn't need a reply. She'd know soon enough.

Unlocking the collar, I held the two ends and bent over her. Wrapping it around her throat, I moved from front to back, positioning myself to fasten it. I kept my voice low and soothing, embracing my cold ruthlessness again. "It's affectionately known as the Weaver Wailer." Using the special clasp—an irreversible clasp—I murmured, "It's your gift from us. Jewels from the best of our mines. You should be proud to wear such wealth."

Nila shivered as the lock snapped into place.

My shoulders relaxed. It was on. It was done.

Her option to leave had just disappeared.

"You're ours now. Want to know why?"

She whimpered, shaking her head.

Gathering her thick black hair, I ignored her plea for ignorance. I'd told her ignorance was bliss—which was true. But my job was to torment her. She had to fully embrace her future.

Breathing gently on her neck, I whispered, "Because once the Weaver Wailer is in place...there's only one way to get it back off."

Nila

"ENOUGH PLAYING, JETHRO, bring her here."

The command burned my ears, turning my false belief I could survive into dirty soot. The fire I'd nursed inside was gone. All the stupid pretending that I could block the worst from damaging my soul disappeared. My little claws had fully retracted into nothing once again.

I was cold. Cold as *him*.

Shut down. Same as him.

Silent. Same as him.

Only one way to get it off.

I swallowed. My head pounded. My hands flew up to tug at the jewelled collar. It was heavy and lifeless and ice. Pure ice. The perfect clarity and flawless sparkle of the diamonds leached into my skin, claiming me, marking me.

Only one way to get it off.

I thought I'd come to terms with my mortality. I thought I'd face the end with my head held high and dry eyes—but that was before they told me the method of my execution. When I thought of death, I pictured…nothing…I had no image of how the end would come.

Now I did.

Only one way to get it off.

I was to be beheaded.

There'd be no sawing off the collar or picking the lock. The way the clasp snapped so resolutely hinted at a one way mechanism. The heavy noose was now mine…an accessory slowly strangling me by diamonds.

It wasn't breakable. But I was. So fragile really, when a single sharp blade could cast me from life into the nether. Diamonds were nature's hardest fortress—the quintessential marriage of unbreakable ice and power.

A new unwanted respect curdled in my stomach. Jethro said his mines. *Their* mines. Diamonds were pure, but the method of collection had a chequered history of death and violence.

They didn't just play the part of untouchables. They *were* untouchable.

No!

My tugging fingers turned frantic. I arched my neck, searching with an edge of insanity for a weakness in the soldered white gold and gemstones. It had to come off.

It has to.

I didn't have the strength to die. I didn't have the martyrdom to let them do this. Not for family. Not for fortune. Not for anything.

I'm weak. I don't want to die!

Jethro grabbed my wrists, effortlessly pulling my arms away from my throat. My eyes opened and all I saw was malevolent stone. There was no compassion in his light-brown eyes. No sympathy or even guilt. How did he have the power to be so close to me—to grow hard wanting me—and know all along my fate?

Only a special person could do that. A person who wasn't born of this world, but brimstone and fire. From *hell*.

I struggled in his hold. The collar settled heavily, spreading its heinous ice. "I was wrong about you."

Jethro placed my hands by my sides, then let me go. He shrugged, running a palm through his thick salt-and-pepper hair. "I've been nothing but forthright and honest from the beginning. You're the one who spun a lie from the truth. *You're the one who ignored everything I was telling you.*"

Turning to face the table, he wrapped a cold arm around my waist. "And now it's time to face the reality of everything you tried to ignore."

Mr. Hawk, with his ridiculous tweed and leather outfit, stubbed out a smouldering cigar. "Did you tell her?"

Jethro stiffened. "I forgot."

His father reclined into the high-backed chair and folded his hands on his stomach. "You were meant to tell her when you put it on. It's called the Weaver Wailer and it belonged to…"

A loud screeching sound exploded in my ears. My stomach rolled. Vertigo spread its nullifying tentacles through my brain.

It's the necklace. The one she wore when she came back the final time.

Jethro looked down, trying to capture my eyes, but I wouldn't do it. I *couldn't* do it. I kept my vision blank, looking resolutely over his shoulder. "I think you've already guessed who it belonged to." Lowering his voice, he whispered, "The last person to wear this collar was your mother. She wore it for two years and twenty-three days before it was…forcibly removed. It carries not only the diamonds of my bloodline, but also blood from yours. We, of course, clean it thoroughly after every owner, but if you look closely, I'm sure you'll see the tarnish of their lives given in return for their crimes."

"Nila, when you're a big girl, you can wear my clothes, shoes, and jewellery, but you have to grow a little taller before that day." My mother laughed, looking down at me on the floor of her walk-in wardrobe. I'd not only raided her jewellery box and draped myself in gemstones, but wore a feather boa with a baggy one piece swimming suit and giant high heels. I thought I looked incredible. For a seven-year-old.

Holding up the pearls around my neck, I said, "Promise? I can have these when I'm your size?"

She ducked, pulling me into a hug. "You can have everything of mine. Why?"

I smiled. I knew the answer to this. "Because you love me."
She nodded. "Because I love you."

The memory came and went, stealing the firm ground beneath my feet and sending me headfirst into nausea. Spirals, loop de loops, and spin-cycles all churned my brain until I didn't know up from down.

It wasn't vertigo this time, but grief.

Crushing, crashing grief. A grief I hadn't suffered, because all my happy memories of her had been blocked by the wall of hatred. She was supposed to be the bad guy for leaving my father. I'd been safe from hurting. Safe from reliving everything with the knowledge of how precious she was. How tragic her life became and for *two years* after she'd left. Two years we didn't try and save her.

The Hawks had stripped her from me and torn away any armour I had against missing her. She wasn't the bad guy. *They* were. They would all die for this. They would rot for eternity. I would find a way.

Please, let me find a way.

I wore a necklace every firstborn woman in my family wore before they were murdered—I was owed serious revenge. Disgusting, painful revenge.

A sob escaped my mouth. I couldn't fight the spinning anymore and doubled over. With a sickening splash, I threw up all over Jethro's shiny black shoes.

"Shit." He jumped back, not that there was much mess. It'd been almost twenty-four hours since I'd eaten—I had nothing to waste or purge. But the dry heaves wouldn't stop racking my frame.

"For fuck's sake, Jet. Get her under control. We don't have all day." Mr. Hawk's voice shouted across the room.

Cold hands grabbed my shoulders, jerking me from bowed to straight. I moaned as my head sloshed with pain.

"Stop embarrassing me," Jethro snarled.

Embarrassing him? Bastard. Arsehole. Son of Satan. I glowered with tear-swimming eyes into Jethro's cold uncompassionate gaze. Something flicked over his gold irises—a dark shadow. That was the only warning I received before his hand came up and struck me around the side of the head.

I thought I was brave. I thought I was strong. But I'd never been struck before. Daniel's slap in the car last night didn't count. This abuse had come from a black place—a place inside Jethro where unsurmountable anger boiled. And it was endless. He may be a glacier on the outside, but in there…in his heart…he steamed with pressuring rage.

Crashing to my knees, I curled my smarting head into my arms. I came from a family who loved each other so much a disappointed look or stern word was enough to break your heart. Physical abuse wasn't something I knew. It wasn't something I could prepare for.

Jethro grabbed my hair, pulling me upright. I held onto his wrists to prevent the tearing pain. My blurry gaze focused on his grey shirt and perfectly creased jeans.

He glared. "You'll clean that up, but for now you have other things to attend to."

Not letting go of my hair, he carted me toward his father. Every step I took, I tried to hide my exposed breasts and ignore the breeze between my naked legs. The pinafore Jethro had put on me barely covered my stomach let alone valuable places. Places I would give my entire design line to have covered. The stupid maid cap tilted to the side, clinging to my tangled hair.

I couldn't count how many men existed around the table, but their eyes never met mine. Most were glued to my chest or mesmerized lower down as I side-shuffled to hide as much of my decency as possible.

But it wasn't just their eyes sending spider legs scurrying over my flesh. It was the huge immaculate paintings of men wearing white wigs, elegant coat and tails, and hunting regalia glaring down from the dark red walls.

Their eyes weren't lifeless but full of disdain—somehow they knew a Weaver was in their midst and the crackling fireplace was useless to stop my chill.

My sentence was to be carried out with ancestors and family heirlooms as witnesses.

The moment we came to a stop beside Mr. Hawk, sitting in his ornate dining chair, Jethro jerked my neck back. His flawless face filled my vision. "You are no longer free. Look. See your future and understand there's no sweet talking, begging, or bargaining your way out of this. You wear the collar. You're ours completely." Jethro's voice was arctic, glittering with power.

The collar cut into my skin. I wanted to spit in his face.

Shoving me toward Mr. Hawk, the old man snaked an arm around my naked waist, tugging me onto his lap.

"Obey and make me proud, Ms. Weaver." Jethro crossed his arms. He shifted to stand behind his father's chair, removing himself from the role of authority, becoming merely a spectator.

He's never called me Nila.

The stupid thought came and went on a heartbeat. Jethro was yet to use my first name.

I shuddered, feeling overwhelmingly sick again.

Jethro was awful but being disowned and handed over to a room of men was worse. I would've given anything to avoid was what about to happen. I would willingly trade all my nights in a bed and return to the kennels. The hounds were loving, kind...warm.

I sat frozen on Mr. Hawk's lap.

His hand rested on my upper thigh, not violating but terrifying. "Now that we all understand each other, I want you to look at something for me, Nila. Then the festivities will begin. Every man you serve, you'll receive another snippet of your history. Only once you've completed your task will you know the entire story and will be free to spend the afternoon either in the steam baths below the house as a reward or in solitary confinement in the dungeons as punishment, depending on how well you please us."

I couldn't understand how my body still functioned. Shock turned my limbs to statues, fear made me mute—I died inside until there was no part of me left. But still my heart kept pumping; my blood kept flowing—staying alive only for their sick pleasure.

The weight of my mother's collar bit into my neck and a question came from no-where. My mother was a Weaver. Her mother before her was a Weaver. But wouldn't they have changed their names according to the surname of their husbands?

I blinked, trying to remember my father's last name.

I can't.

"You look confused. I'll permit you to ask a question before we proceed," Mr. Hawk said, settling me higher on his knee.

I fought my cringe, struggling to formulate the words. "My mother's maiden name was Weaver, but she would've changed it when she got married." I glanced at Jethro behind his father's chair. He tilted his chin, looking down his nose.

Mr. Hawk shook his head. "That son of mine hasn't explained anything has he." Twisting in the seat, he glanced at Jethro. "What exactly have you been doing? You know information is what grants us control. We're the ones in the right. How can she hope to accept her situation if you keep her in the dark?"

Jethro clenched his jaw but remained silent.

Rolling his eyes, Mr. Hawk faced me again and smiled. "I'll give you a brief history lesson, then you must begin your duties." Reaching up, he tugged the maid's cap on my head.

Every inch of me crawled, but I didn't move away. I was hungry for knowledge. Starving to know just how they continued to control my family with no fear of police interference or retribution.

Mr. Hawk reclined, his thumb drawing small circles on my upper thigh. "It all began with one man, who you'll find out about in a little bit. He had children, gracing them all with the

Weaver name. Now, from that day on, the power of the family name travelled with the firstborn girl. No matter if she married, divorced, or suddenly wanted to change her name to something whimsical, she wasn't permitted. Whoever she married, it was a condition that the *man* change his name so that their offspring always bore the Weaver name and continued the line of succession of the debt."

Why did they do it? Why keep a name that only brought misery? My mind hurt trying to understand the Hawk's power.

"You, I believe, are the seventh woman to be taken. And the claiming can happen anywhere between the ages of eighteen and twenty-six."

"You have rules on ruining someone's life?"

His forehead furrowed. "What do you think we're doing, Nila? *Everything* we're doing is following a strict set of rules—laid out in utmost simplicity and must be followed."

"If you're following rules, then follow the rules of today's society. You think I accept what you're telling me? That all of this is *legal?*" I spat the last word. "You think its common place to threaten my family, steal me away, and imprison me with a collar of diamonds that won't come off until I die? You're completely insane. And wrong. And—"

"No one—especially a Weaver—has the right to speak to me like that." Mr. Hawk's fingernails bit into my thigh. "What part are you not understanding, girl? We haven't threatened your family—they are under observeillance to ensure their best behaviour. We didn't steal you away—you came voluntarily, remember? And as for the collar—you should be proud to wear it. It's the most treasured piece in the Hawks antiquities."

I bit my lip as his fingernails pierced harder.

His voice dropped the scholarly softness, sliding into strictness. "I see you need more concrete evidence. Fine. The diamonds you wear are worth millions. The diamonds we've sourced have been used to trade, buy services, bribe officials, own prime ministers, even control diplomats and royalty. No one is above the allure of a flawless diamond, Ms. Weaver.

Everyone has a price. Lucky for us, we can *afford* any price."

His tone sharpened. "Does that answer your rude question?"

What response could I give? There was nothing I could say or do to ignore my entire situation. They might have some misplaced belief that they were in the right—but that didn't matter. Because they owned the very people I would need to save me.

My shoulders dipped.

Mr. Hawk grinned. "Glad you're coming to your senses. Don't under estimate us, Nila Weaver. We've had the law on our side for hundreds of years. We *still* have the law on our side and that won't change. You are nothing more than a single woman who left the world's spotlight because she fell in love. You are already consumed and forgotten."

His fingernails stopped slicing my leg; he patted me gently. "I apologise that my son didn't inform you of this. It's his job to be implicitly open with you. To ensure you accept your new standing quickly." He threw a glare at Jethro behind us.

Jethro locked his jaw, his eyes unreadable.

Mr. Hawk bounced me on his knee. "Now, no more questions. Serve my Diamond brothers and earn your right to more information."

My heart shot up my throat. "Serve them how?"

Mr. Hawk shook his head. "Ah, I just told you, no more questions. I have no doubt Jethro would've been rather firm on *that* instruction. Silence is the key to pleasing us." He pinched my lips together. "Don't say a word until we permit it, and you'll be rewarded."

I'm to be a blow-up doll with no voice or soul?

Looking down, I fought against the urge to tear my face from his grip.

He didn't let me go. And I couldn't keep fighting the urge. So I did the only thing I could. Slowly, I nodded, losing another battle against the trickling tears cascading silently down my cheeks. They continued their unhindered sad journey down my neck, through the collar, to my naked nipples below.

The sun glinted through the window, blinding me for a second on the diamond pin in Jethro's shirt. His eyes were tight and narrowed, glaring at the room of leather-jacketed men; his face resolute and frozen.

Freeing me, Mr. Hawk ordered, "Lean forward, and retrieve the first bit of parchment."

I sat unmoving. I didn't want to wriggle on his lap. I didn't want to give any reason for things to grow or hands to grope.

Jethro lashed out from behind, catching me by surprise. He didn't hit me, but grabbed my diamond collar and snapped a leash to the back. Tugging the restraint, he muttered, "Lesson one. You'll do as your told the *second* you're told it. Otherwise, you'll choke until you do."

He moved to the back of the chair, leaving my line of sight. The moment he was gone, the pressure on the collar increased, digging into my larynx, cutting off my air supply.

Just let him strangle you.

It would be easier.

But as my body crushed against Mr. Hawk from the pressure, and the natural instinct to fight took over, I knew I couldn't be so weak. There was no point in being stupid. If I was plane-wrecked in a jungle, I would obey the law of the wild—doing absolutely anything to survive.

Wasn't this the same thing?

I was in a den of beasts and they were trying to help me by teaching me their law. If I obeyed, I would live. Entirely simple. Stupidly simple.

No sound, Nila. Not one word. Switch off. Retreat into that spot inside and get through this.

I could do it by adapting, by learning. I refused to be hurt for punishments I could avoid.

Jethro sensed my acquiescence at the same time as his father. I didn't know what gave me away—the slouching of my shoulders, the soft puff of sadness? Regardless, they knew I wouldn't fight. They'd won.

Jethro released the pressure on my throat, removing the leash and dangling it over the back of the chair as he moved back to his position. Mr. Hawk angled my face, pressing a wet kiss on my cheek. "Good girl. You're learning."

I didn't even flinch. I was as cold as his son.

Embrace it.

Locking eyes with Jethro, I kept myself anchored while his father's hand slipped inside the stupid pinafore and found my breast.

Jethro gritted his teeth, but never stopped glaring into my blank gaze.

I tensed, willing every molecule to stay frigid and unattached. There was freedom in drifting—as I'd learned in the kennel—and I let my mind go.

I would be Jethro and remain stone cold on the outside. But inside I would be Kite and cut the strings of my soul— soaring where they'd never touch me.

No matter what they did.

My head bowed as Mr. Hawk pressed up, grinding a hard cock against my naked arse. "Read the parchment."

My hair fell in a thick black curtain, obscuring half of the men who watched with eager eyes.

My hands didn't shake as I reached for the parchment. I lowered my eyes to read. I was silently amazed at how collected and aloof I seemed. Shocked that I'd so easily turned off. What did that say about me? I'd just learned about my mother. Spent the night with a pack of dogs. *Am I really that adaptable?* Or was shock to blame?

The parchment used to be whole—it was age-stained, blood-marked, and torn. Glancing upright, I noticed the remaining pieces scattered around the table. A treasure hunt to read what would be my sentence.

Not every man had a piece, but at a quick count, I guessed four to five shards of secret-tarnished paper were out there, waiting for me to read.

Looking back to the parchment in my hands, my eyes

landed on the crest I'd grown fast to recognise of hawks, women, and diamonds. It took pride of place at the top of the letter with intricate calligraphy and penmanship.

Taking a deep breath, I read.

On this date, the eighteenth day, of the eighth month, of the year of our Lord fourteen-seventy-two, we hereby convene to settle the unsightly claims and forthwith family disruptions between Percy Weaver and Bennett Hawk.

We call upon the royal sovereignty to grace this binding agreement upon the two houses, to put aside flagitious slander, and immoral actions, and settle this as gentlemen.

As esquire over this binding estate, I have mention Percy Weaver and family, including church-sanctified marriage to Mary Weaver, and his thrice offspring of two boys and one girl are also governed by the degree found today, or they shall hang by the neck until dead for heinous crimes found unjustifiable by the court of England so help me God.

It ended.

I stopped reading but didn't move. Not a breath. Not a fidget. It was true then. My family had done something to justify all of this.

But what could be so awful to earn a contract spanning generations of repayments?

Mr. Hawk bounced me again, tweaking my nipple. "Finished?"

My heart neither fluttered nor sank. I was flying free—escaped from this unfolding nightmare.

"Intrigued? Want to know the rest?" His fingers twisted harder, but I didn't care. All I cared about was finding out more.

Ignoring his touch, I breathed for the first time and nodded. As much as I didn't want to get close to the other men, curiosity burned. I was desperate to read more torn pages and solve the mystery of my lineage.

Why did father never say anything? Why did he raise me to think we were good people?

That question would probably never be answered.

Mr. Hawk placed his hands on my hips, hoisting me from his lap. I stood with my eyes cast downward. Silent and waiting.

He smiled in encouragement. "Behaving well so far. Let's see if you can keep it up." Waving toward the overladen sideboard full of hors d'oeuvres, fish dishes, meat dishes, roast vegetables, and desserts, he said, "You're our waitress for this little get together. Please be so kind as to serve our meal. You'll receive a token of thanks from each of the Black Diamond brothers and earn the right to finish your reading."

My legs moved before my brain registered. The primal part of me taking over to jump to the task. I might be a naïve woman who didn't know how to jerk a man off, but I was a businesswoman at heart. I'd been around strict shop buyers, ditzy models, and sulking catalogue owners. I'd learned how to adapt and sell my work.

This was no different.

I had to adapt and sell myself.

Make him care. Make him feel.

My eyes flew to Jethro. Was it possible? Could I break his ice and find a man deep inside—a man who I could seduce, beguile, and ultimately use to stay alive?

Am I that strong?

Mr. Hawk tapped my behind as I skirted the back of his chair. Jethro didn't move, granting a small space for me to pass.

I hunched into myself, preparing for whatever cruelty he had planned.

His body twitched. The perfect lines of muscle and masculinity once again making me despise his natural beauty. An unwilling rush shot through my system at the memory of him fingering me.

He'd wanted me in that moment and it had nothing to do with debts or pain. It'd been pleasurable, confusing, and awkward but…maybe there was something I could work with.

The idea to seduce Jethro flowered quickly. The bloom

wasn't fresh like the bud of a rose but *black*. The unfurling petals dripped with filth, sprouting from a place I never wanted to acknowledge. He belonged to a family who ruined mine. He had no compassion. No heart.

How could I make him care when stone was utterly heartless?

I'll try, though. I had nothing left to lose.

I could be their ward, to be tormented on a daily basis, for years. I would be his toy for however long he wanted. Time could change anything if the elements conspired with me. A mountain ultimately had to give way to the sea if hammered by its salty waves.

I'll be that wave.

Jethro cleared his throat, deliberately stepping forward. His large frame pressed against mine, causing my body to twist and brush my naked breasts against him.

"Oops," he breathed.

I didn't look into his eyes. I couldn't stand to look at him. All of this was his doing and I refused to let him unsettle me anymore. "Don't touch me," I whisper-hissed.

His hand lashed out, slinking up my pinafore and tweaking the same nipple his father had. "Silence." He bowed his head to mine. "And you loved me touching you. Stop being a little liar, Ms. Weaver."

Gritting my teeth, I darted away, tearing his fingers from my breast. I breathed hard when I reached the sideboard. So much food.

My stomach scrunched into a hunger ache.

So what I was naked? So what over twenty men waited to do who knew what to me? It didn't matter. Because my life hinged on throwing away normal and embracing the crazy I now lived with.

I would meet them in hell and play their horrid games. *I'll come out the victor.*

Grabbing a tiered platter of pâté, crusty bread, and pickled vegetables, my mouth watered.

I'm so hungry.

My stomach growled, sending spasms of pain. I'd never gone this long without food, and the lack of sugars and vitamins faded the edges of my vision. My fingers whispered over a piece of roasted potato. Just one little taste…

"Hurry up," Mr. Hawk ordered.

Shaking my head from the overwhelming need to shove a handful of delicious looking food into my mouth, I turned to face the table. I'd never waitressed before, but I guessed the man in charge would get first choice.

That means passing him again.

Holding tight to the platter, I held my head high, and made my way past Jethro. His mouth twitched as he once again blocked my path. I kept my lips tight together, not looking at the challenge in his eyes.

"Not interested in me anymore, Ms. Weaver?" he purred.

Mr. Hawk looked over his chair and pointed at me, then placed his finger over his lips in the universal 'hush' sign. A non-so-subtle reminder that I wasn't permitted to speak.

When I didn't respond. Jethro smiled. "I'm impressed."

He might terrify me, but he needed to know I wouldn't give up. I had plans for him, and I wouldn't be so easily cowed. Plus, he had my vomit on his shoes, he shouldn't be so smug.

I let myself glance into his golden eyes. *You don't scare me.*

His capricious demeanour shifted slightly, a silent message glowing in his gaze. *Give me time.*

He let me pass without another word.

Breathing shallowly, I came to a standstill beside Mr. Hawk. He nodded, choosing a selection from the platter. "Good girl. You may now serve the rest of the table. Left to right, if you please."

Straightening, I forced myself to truly look at the men before me—the gauntlet of masculinity I had to travel through to reach my destination.

My heart raced; a cold sweat broke out down my spine. *Stay cold. Stay free. And you'll get through this.*

I placed one foot, then another. My heartbeat ratcheted as I came to a stop beside a large man. He had orange hair and a tattoo snaking up his neck.

My vision wobbled; I tottered to the left as a small wave of vertigo reminded me I'd been stable up to this point thanks to a miracle. Orange Tattoo shot out an arm, preventing me from slamming into the table.

He grinned. "Steady, I won't bite." He brought me close, smiling so deep a dimple formed. "I'll lick though."

Before I could move, his tongue landed on my thigh, licking long and slow like a giant animal.

What?!

I squirmed, almost dropping the tray. His grip was absolute, holding me firm until he'd tasted his full. The rush of vertigo turned to nausea. The sickly scent of my previous sickness didn't help my stomach from rolling like a shipwreck.

Letting me go, I stumbled and tried to rub away the glisten of wetness from his awful mouth. It only transferred to my naked elbow.

Orange Tattoo beamed, licked his lips, and took a selection of breads and pickles. "Thank you, Ms. Weaver."

I spun to face Mr. Hawk.

This couldn't be true. He expected me to let this happen. From *everyone?*

Mr. Hawk chewed thoughtfully, raising an eyebrow, daring me to speak.

My lips parted—to demand to know what happened. Was that the token of gratitude he spoke of? A *lick?*

My chest puffed, sending a wash of embarrassment through me. Not only was I naked but I had to permit them *licking* me!

Mr. Hawk pursed his lips, waiting for me to explode.

He'll punish you. Don't ask. Do. Not. Snap.

It took more courage and energy than I had. But I managed to suck in a breath and release the stress swirling in my system. I had too many other things to focus on to care

about an unorthodox dinner soirée.
No speaking.
I had to pretend I had no tongue. Otherwise, waitressing would be the least of my problems.
Glancing back at the men, they grinned, knowing I had no choice but to continue.
Jethro's voice ghosted behind me like a dark cloud. "You're the main course, Ms. Weaver. Each brother gets a taste—anywhere he chooses. You'd be wise to allow it."
My heart thundered. *Anywhere?*
But if it was just a lick—was that so bad? Perhaps this dinner party might not be as awful as I'd feared. A lick I could tolerate. A touch I could handle. Full penetration would drive my mind from its sanctuary straight to an asylum.
It was as if Jethro knew that. Pushing me, little by little, past my comfort zone.
I moved to the next leather-jacketed man. This one was skinny but had an edge of violence. His shaved head shone as he helped himself to the food before placing his finger in the top of my pinafore and pulling me down to his level.
His tongue lashed out, tracing my cheekbone all the way to my ear.
Shuddering, I swallowed back my repulsion.
You can handle it.
The moment he'd finished, he said, "Thank you, Ms. Weaver."
What did they want for me—permission that it was okay? That I was *grateful?*
Standing upright, I struggled to move. Struggled to keep going when I knew how many more licks I'd have to earn before it was over.
"Proceed, Ms. Weaver. Don't disappoint me." Jethro's gravelly voice invaded my ears. Damn him. Damn all of this.
Swallowing hard, I moved to the next.
He was handsome. Quite like Jethro in a stockier, less devilish kind of way. He had dark hair with flecks of grey and a

bird of prey tattooed on his forearm.

Never taking his eyes from mine, he took a few items, then hooked a strong arm around my waist and pushed up my maid's uniform. His lips pressed a kiss on my hipbone, the wet tease of a tongue hidden by the warm pressure of his mouth.

Every inch of me revolted but I didn't flinch.

Smirking, he let me go. "Thank you, Ms. Weaver."

It was the smirk that gave him away.

He's another Hawk.

The man nodded, sensing my connection to his pedigree. "I'm the second brother," he said softly. "I doubt you know my name seeing as Jethro gets to have all the fun—but I'll tell you—so you know who to scream for when my older brother goes too far." He crooked his finger, hinting for me to move closer.

Despite myself, I bent. There was something about this brother. Something different.

His light-brown eyes—a Hawk family trait it seemed—crinkled at the corners. "I'm Kestrel." Pointing at the tattoo on his arm, he added, "Like the bird."

"Leave her alone, Kes. Other brothers want a turn." Jethro's demand snapped from behind.

Kestrel chuckled. "Easy there, Jet. Only playing with my food." He sat back, motioning me to continue.

How many sons did Mr. Hawk have? How many must I submit to when Jethro had had enough of me? I didn't have the mental protection to sleep with an entire family of evilness.

My eyes didn't linger on him and I wasn't permitted to speak, but I wanted to know more about him. I wanted to know why I had a sense of kinship—no matter how slight.

Tense, I darted around his chair, moving to my next customer.

The next man had piercings in his eyebrow and lower lip. Blue-black hair, so similar to Vaughn's, tore my heart out as he bent his head over my arm and dragged a pointed tongue toward my elbow.

V.

Tears threatened. V was everything to me. I couldn't stand to think of him while this happened. I should've messaged him back. I was cruel to leave him in distress.

Closing my eyes, I put one foot in front of the other, moving toward the next man.

And then the next.

And the next.

Each one thanked me once they'd tasted, acting like gentlemen rather the lair of monsters they truly were.

With every lick, I froze, standing tense and hating while they dragged their saliva all over my skin.

Thankfully, the lack of hunger tripped time, merging the men and tongues into a merry-go-round of nightmares. I lost track of who licked where, hiding myself away and focusing on the weight of my platter growing lighter and lighter.

But not one person tasted my breasts or pussy.

It sent me into a state of uncomfortable awareness. They were men. Taunting a woman who they'd been given permission to taste. Why hadn't they gone for the prized locations?

The unknowing and waiting sent my skin crawling more than their eager tongues.

The next man I served was older with a greying moustache and wispy hair. He licked my neck, nuzzling my hair before taking his fill of food.

I went to move, in a trance, to the next diner.

But the older man captured my hip and presented me with the next part of the parchment.

My trance evaporated, leaving me hungry for information. This was why I permitted this. I let myself be governed by history. The double meaning of the thought didn't escape me. *You were taken because of history. You're staying because of history.*

The diamonds of my collar bit into my neck in agreeance.

Placing the platter on the table, I removed myself from the twenty-first century and proceeded to be swept to 1472.

For actions committed by Percy Weaver and his entourage of well-to-do associates, he stands judged and wanting. His life is determined by the grace of Bennett Hawk who states the following comeuppance:
Monetary compensation
Public apology
And most of all, bodily retribution

What a bastard. He couldn't let some petty grievance go? *He did save the entire family from hanging.* Somehow, he'd kept Percy Weaver and my ancestors from swinging on a rope, and in a way, I had to be grateful. Grateful to a man who'd saved my bloodline but stolen my future at the same time.

If this document had never been agreed upon, I would never have been born. No one past Percy and Mary would've existed. It was hard to hate someone who'd granted life, but easy to hate them for stealing countless of those lives generations later.

"Keep going, Ms. Weaver," Jethro purred.

My head snapped up.

He stood there, wrapped in his horrible silence.

I wanted to glower. I wanted to do something idiotic and stick my tongue out at him. But there was no point making him hate me more than he already did. The moment I could charge my phone, I would Google every enticing come-hithers a woman could make.

I'll seduce him.

I'd enjoyed seeing his impeccable control snap by the stables. I loved that I was the one to do it.

I'll make him care.

I would turn this travesty into a prophecy by weaving my Weaver magic over a Hawk.

With strength building in my heart, I grabbed my tray.

Moving forward on unsteady knees, I looked greedily at the next piece of paper. It sat coyly in the centre of the table, beckoning.

The next man to taste me was a young boy, barely out of his teens. His touch was gentle, tongue barely licking. He was my favourite from the table.

After another two licks, I hoped I deserved the next scrap of parchment, but no one gave it to me. My heart sank as I completed a full rotation, squeezing my eyes as each tongue inched closer to the places I wished were covered.

I couldn't stop shivering when I placed the empty platter on the sideboard. Resting my palms on the hard surface, I breathed deep. Tears pressed on the back of my eyes, disgust rolled in my stomach growling with desperate hunger. This was torture on so many levels. Delivering food to well-fed men all the while they feasted on me, too.

"The main course, if you will, Nila," Mr. Hawk muttered.

I looked over my shoulder. He sat there, running his fingers through his goatee. His golden eyes, so like Jethro's, held no patience or tolerance but his lips tilted in mirth. He was enjoying this.

Of course he was. They *all* were.

Including my main tormentor.

Pushing off from the sideboard, I collected a large silver tray of chicken and asparagus. Keeping my eyes down, I deliberately kept the tray high and outstretched, giving me a shield in which to pass Jethro.

Not that it helped.

His arm shot out, stopping me. I cursed the familiarity of his touch. Screamed at the horrible way my body remembered the pleasure he'd granted by the stables. I wanted nothing from him. Especially the memory of his fingers.

I glared into his eyes. *Stay silent.*

It was hard.

I had so much I wanted to say. So much to yell. The side of my head still throbbed from his strike; my ego still hurt from not knowing how to jerk him off the way he desired. He made me feel like a rejected little girl.

Bowing close, he whispered in my ear, "I'm enjoying

watching you be so obedient, Ms. Weaver. And your silence..." He brushed my hair away from my cheek, fingertips lingering on my neck. "...is making me hard."

I sucked in a gasp, looking to the front of his trousers despite myself. The outline of his massive cock that terrified me—more than his hands, temper, or god-awful silence—stood firm and bulging against his jeans.

He smiled. "Keep up the good work and you might get two rewards this evening." His eyes darkened. "Because we both know you want me to finish what I started."

My gasp turned to a growl. I couldn't fathom how my stomach swooped even while sickness swirled. Damn my traitorous body for finding his evil beauty attractive.

Are you sure you want to seduce him just for protection? I hated the question. I hated that I didn't have an answer.

Jerking away from him, I stalked toward my starting position. Standing beside Mr. Hawk, I served him first. The moment he'd taken a few morsels, I moved to leave, but he pinched my pinafore, keeping me still.

His eyes met mine and I knew, just *knew*, this serving round wouldn't be my arms, neck, or hips up for a taste. This would be worse. *Much* worse.

"Face me, girl," he ordered.

My teeth chattered, but I slowly did as he requested.

"Lean down."

Closing my eyes, I obeyed.

His hot breath clouded over my chest before a wet, warm mouth latched onto my nipple. A graze of teeth, a swipe of a tongue—it all drove me to the pinnacle. The pinnacle where I knew I would burn in hell for not only permitting it, but for the tiny flutter of need that had burst into life while his son drove his finger inside me.

My head pounded as I shoved the betrayal away. I was the one who betrayed myself. I was the one not strong enough to fight Jethro. He'd won the moment I saw him and let my need for touch consume me.

Tears tickled my spine and the moment Mr. Hawk pulled way, I ran.

I didn't get far.

Orange Tattoo, who sat next to Mr. Hawk caught me, holding me tight. "Now, now. You're doing so well. Don't ruin it." His large hand splayed on my shoulder blades, jerking me to his sitting level. With a tight smile, his mouth latched onto my other nipple.

I whimpered as his large soppy lips sucked. He took his time, swirling his tongue around the hard bud, before letting go in a loud slurp.

I stood shaking as he selected some chicken and sent me on my way.

I can't do this.

Self-pity filled my empty stomach, and I stood frozen to the thick burgundy carpet.

"Move, Ms. Weaver," Jethro murmured.

My body swayed to obey but everything inside rebelled. I didn't care Mr. Hawk had eloquently described my cage with the use of diamonds and debts. I didn't care that I had no choice but to do as I was told.

I just couldn't do it.

My eyes flew wide as Jethro's hands landed on my shoulders. He spun me to face him, breathing hard. "Do. It. Now." The force of his command buckled my knees. I dropped my head.

Silently, Jethro stormed me forward, presenting me to the next man. The platter wobbled in my hands but I stood upright while a vile mouth suckled on my breast.

Once it was over, Jethro manhandled me to the next, whispering in my ear, "Make me come back and show you how to behave, and I won't be nice. You still cling to the ideology that you're better than us. That any moment this will be over." His teeth nipped at my ear. "That's torture because it's false. It won't happen. Accept it and be done with the past. Accept it and embrace everything we're giving you."

Shoving me forward, he patted my backside. "I can be nice if you give me reason to be, Ms. Weaver. Try me by behaving for the rest of the luncheon."

I didn't watch as he left, resuming his standing position behind his father's chair.

I can be nice.

Bullshit he could be nice. But the sooner I obeyed, the sooner it was over.

So...I obeyed.

Mouths.

Fingers.

Tongues and teeth.

They all tasted. They all groped.

I thought the first course was hard. I'd clung to the morals of how wrong it was for so many men to treat one woman so unfairly.

This course did things to me I wished I could deny. Fat lips, thin lips, hot mouths, cool mouths. They all not only *took* from me but *gave* something in return.

A horrible realisation that my body was taking over.

My horror sank like a rock every time a man had a new taste. Slowly my stomach fluttered; my insides rebelling against the melting that occurred.

The men didn't care countless mouths had been on my skin. They took turns between my left and right nipples, nibbling, sucking. I wished they'd bite. I willed them to hurt me—*something* to prove how vile they were.

But each one—old, young, trim, overweight—they all loved me. They adoringly suckled. They moaned with such deep appreciation, I struggled to remember this was by force not by choice. I felt as if I granted them a gift.

A gift they truly appreciated.

Don't. Don't buy into the mindfuckery.

Even my inner voice turned slightly breathless, a lot confused, and edging toward acceptance.

I grew lightheaded as I trudged from man to man. I didn't

make eye contact with any of them. I became listless. Numb. Apart from a tiny spark tugging on the invisible cord from my nipples to my core. I wished it wasn't so. I craved to remain unaffected.

But slowly they turned me from intellectual businesswoman to trembling plaything.

Slowly, I grew wet.

Sharp teeth dragged my attention through the blackness that'd become my soul, back to reality.

I looked into the eyes of Daniel.

The mellow trance I'd been lulled into snapped like a rubber band. I no longer found any acceptance or lusty appeal, only hollow rage.

"It's not much fun licking a woman when she isn't paying attention," he sneered.

My heartbeat flew terrorised around my chest. My nipple throbbed from where he'd bitten me.

Licking his lips, he added, "You taste good, Weaver, but I'm looking forward to the next course."

My heart promptly shot itself and splattered against the floor.

The next course.

No. No. No. No.

"Here. You earned this." Shoving another piece of parchment my way, I forced back my tears.

Moving awkwardly, I placed the empty tray on the sideboard, then returned to Daniel's side. My skin broke out in goosebumps being so close, but he dangled the parchment like a present I desperately wanted.

Taking it, I couldn't hide my shakes this time. My aloofness and spirit were gone, replaced by a brittle shaking leaf.

A leaf that was turned on and damp.

Upon reflection of his crimes, Percy Weaver hereby submits to this esquire's ruling and moves to action the latest degree formulated in this very chamber by Bennett Hawk. The death warrant upon the heads of the Weaver House will be eradicated and burned upon signature of this newly drafted document. Terms forthcoming...

That was it?

Tears spurted from my eyes. I'd let countless men suck on my breasts for no more than a tease?

How could they?

How could *I*?

How could I allow my body to react to their foul ministrations? I hated myself. I hated that I couldn't hide my weakness or the stupid hormones I'd spent my whole life ignoring.

My knees wobbled and I almost folded like an accordion to the floor.

"You pass out and you won't like what you find when you awake." Jethro's voice cut through my grief.

Anger battled away my tears, nursing a new warmth inside. A warmth born of rage rather than flimsy passion. This burned hotter; it licked with orange flames, abolishing my hunger and weakness.

I was fed by anger. I smouldered with hate. I became stronger because of it. It gave me power to continue, but also stole my safety of acceptance. I hissed and scalded with liveliness. I couldn't switch off.

"The next course, Ms. Weaver," Jethro commanded from his position at the head of the table. Balling my hands, I threw away the parchment and stalked to the sideboard.

Dessert.

I knew what would happen.

I can't do this.

You will *do this.*

In my rage, I made a reckless decision. I was at war with my body—why not step over the battle line and join them? Why not embrace it? It was yet another tool—another lesson. If I embraced the new feelings inside, I would be better equipped at chipping away at Jethro's cold exoskeleton of ice and burrowing my way into his warmth.

I would make him care.

I would pleasure him.

Then I would kill him.

My legs scissored together. Everything inside curled deeper into hiding. The moment I went near the table, I would lose all control. I didn't trust my body. It overpowered me every time. And it sucked to be in this mess with a traitor.

Get it over and done with.

Taking a deep breath, I collected my last course.

Passing Jethro with a gilded tray of mini éclairs, bon bons, and trifles, I kept my eyes down. He'd torment me, no doubt.

Sure enough, his arm wrapped around my shoulders, forcing me to face him. His breathing was slightly uneven; his voice lost a tiny shred of chilliness. "Get through this, and I'll reward you. I'll be kind, because you deserve it." Pressing a possessive kiss on my cheek, he whispered, "I'll wipe it all away."

I was struck dumb by the rare and scarily beautiful glimpse at a man I didn't know existed. But then I blinked as Jethro's ice slid back into place, a grim smirk on his lips. "My offer only stands as long as you don't speak, act out, or disappoint me."

Unwinding his arm, he shoved me toward his father.

Almost drunkenly, I moved toward Mr. Hawk. My stomach quivered with trepidation; my heart was prey running frantically for its life.

Mr. Hawk smiled, holding up another piece of paper. "Here. Your last one until you've completed this final service. I think you deserve it, don't you?" His eyes raked down the front of my ridiculous maid's uniform. The cap had stayed in place—how, I didn't know.

Patting my arse, he added, "I must admit you refrained beautifully, even your mother who was my favourite, didn't do so elegantly at her first dinner party."

I ignored that, latching onto the parchment.

Mr. Hawk motioned me to put the tray on the table, before handing over the small piece.

Percy Weaver and family hereby acknowledge his agreeance to the one and only term set forth by Bennett Hawk. In accordance with the law, both parties have agreed that the paperwork is binding, unbreakable, and incontestable from now and forever. Details and parties of both signatures are displayed on the enclosed verified document, henceforth known as the Debt Inheritance.

My eyes met his.

If only I had the rest. I would scream and give up the charade of obedience. I was done. I would take pain to avoid what was about to happen. I would take pain rather than pleasure because then I would still know myself. The longer this went on, the less in-tune I was with the girl I'd been.

Too many feelings. Too many sensors. Too many rabbit-holes with too many right and wrongs.

You're giving up so soon? They killed your mother! They've broken your father's heart. Could I not stomach some unpleasantness and confusion in order to find a way to repay them?

Disappointment weighed my heart. I thought I'd have more endurance.

No. I won't give in.

This is nothing. Be that kite. Cut your strings again.

Bracing my shoulders, I moved closer to Mr. Hawk without being asked.

His eyes widened, then a grin spread his lips. "Good girl, indeed." Bowing his head, his arm wrapped around my waist, tilting me back a little. "You're proving to be a testament to my son's training."

My waist height was almost perfect for a lowered mouth to latch onto the front part of my sex.

And that was when I felt the strangest, wettest, alluring, *disgusting* thing of my life.

His tongue slid along my clit, wriggling softly, drenching

me in saliva.

My stomach clenched, my hands balled, and I wobbled in his arms.

The disgusting element didn't leave. I waited for my body to betray me, to *like* it, but all I felt was grotesque impatience for it to be over.

And then…it was.

My first experience with a tongue down below, and it'd been done by a man older than my father. If I didn't have an empty stomach, I would've thrown up all over again. There was nothing sexy or erotic about that.

Tapping my behind, he murmured, "Proceed."

Swallowing hard, I collected the dessert tray and crossed the small distance to Orange Tattoo. He crooked his finger, beckoning me closer. Locking my jaw, I held the desserts high and did as he requested. His orange hair tickled my thighs as he leaned down, running his tongue over the private bundle of nerves.

Luckily for me, I wasn't sensitive, nor did I enjoy it.

Once he'd taken his trifle and tasted his fill, I left to serve the next.

And the next.

And the next.

Some men forced my legs to spread, angling their faces deep. Some men barely touched me, their hot breath wafting between my thighs.

I would like to say I managed to turn my brain off—to do what I promised and fly free, but every tongue kept me locked in the world I lived in. Every lick made my body turn to stone while my tummy twisted and ached from clenching.

I delivered dessert, but I was the ultimate sweet. The men took their time, firm fingers holding my hips, dragging their foul tongues. And after every violation, they'd wipe their glistening mouths and say, "Thank you, Ms. Weaver."

Thank you.

As if their appreciation was enough to stop me from

feeling like dirt. Their treatment never changed. They remained courteous and gentle. Obeying boundaries and not doing anything but licking me in a place they had no right.

Their pleasantness made all of this seem so normal. So terribly normal. And my hatred slowly switched back to acceptance. The small flutter I'd felt from my nipples being sucked returned—frightful, tentative, but softening my hate tongue by tongue.

They weren't hurting me. They weren't making me do anything that had the potential to shatter my mind.

They just tasted.

A little taste.

That's all.

And I didn't fight.

Not at all.

I'm wet.

By the time I came to Daniel, my legs were drenched and the trimmed hair I meticulously maintained was mattered with droplets of Diamond brotherhood.

My hands were balled around the tray; my jaw tight and aching. Because no matter my good intentions—they'd won. They'd caused my body to have a reaction, and I was soaking.

The strange ache that Jethro had conjured was back, pulsing deep in my core. The flicker of tongues and gentle tastes frustrated me and I hated, *positively hated*, that I had to fight my hips from pressing harder against them.

I'd begun the service uptight but now I was *wound* tight. Seeking something. Seeking relief.

Daniel pushed his chair back, angling me physically between his spread hips. With a malicious glint in his eyes, he pushed me back with a firm palm between my breasts. "Fuck the stupid rule."

I gasped as his mouth latched around my clit. The suction of his mouth made my body twist with oversensitivity. He wasn't playful or respectful like the rest of the men. He knew what he wanted and he took.

Hard.

The ache wound tighter and tighter, clawing its way toward relief.

I squeezed my eyes. I couldn't look at the men watching. I couldn't do anything but breathe and get through it. And I definitely couldn't look up where a small growl came, masked with silence.

It was nothing more than a growl.

But it resonated in my bones with knowledge.

Jethro.

The few seconds that each man had taken seemed much longer in Daniel's arms. Suddenly, I cried out, jerking hard.

The tip of his tongue probed my entrance, trying to enter me.

No one had done that. They'd behaved with some unspoken rule to taste but not devour.

Fuck the stupid rule.

Daniel's voice repeated in my head. Had there been guidelines on how I was to be treated?

Everything we're doing is following a strict set of rules—laid out in utmost simplicity and must be followed.

I recalled what Mr. Hawk had said.

He had rules meant to ruin me but also…protect me?

Daniel tried again, his fingers biting into me painfully.

Then, I was wrenched away.

Torn free of his grip with a slice of his fingernails and dragged to the end of the table. The empty dessert tray went flying, clanging against the floor.

My legs tripped, sending me colliding with a body I'd been so intimate with only hours before.

The crash of the tray cut through the room like a loud cymbal. But no one said a word.

The moment Jethro dragged me to the head of the table opposite Mr. Hawk, he shoved the largest of all parchments into my hands. His eyes were dark, face tight. "Here, read it."

Breathing fast, trying hard to forget about the sticky saliva between my legs and the sensation of having his brother's tongue trying to enter me, I took the tattered age-stained scroll.

Jethro scowled, keeping a small distance between us. His coldness buffeted me, sending ice scattering over my bare arms. He looked pissed off—furious, yet there was something there that made my stomach twist.

Whatever game we'd played, whatever war we'd started back at the stables, wasn't finished. He knew it. I knew it. And the knowledge sent power thrilling through my veins.

Leaning close, he hissed, "Stop staring at me, Ms. Weaver. I gave you a request." Tapping the scroll in my palm, he snapped, "Read. It."

Tearing my eyes from his, I obeyed.

The intricate border caught my attention first. Along with a design of vines and filigree, the words *bound, indebted, owned* were entwined in red ink.

The calligraphy of ancestors past sentenced me to a life worse than death. My rights had been taken. My life stolen. My body no longer mine.

18th August 1472
Signed and witness by Esq John Law
Matter between Weaver versus Hawk
Known forthwith as the Debt Inheritance

This hereby concludes all debate and conversation and puts forth a binding debt. Council has been provided along with sovereign approval for such an agreement.

As set in this chamber, I have witnessed the signatures of both parties of House Weaver and House Hawk, along with their significant entourage and companions.

The debt states as follows.

Percy Weaver hereby solemnly swears to present his firstborn girl-child, Sonya Weaver, to the firstborn son of Bennett Hawk, known as William Hawk. This will nullify all unrest and unpleasantries until such a time as a new generation comes to pass.

This debt will not only bind the current occupancies of the year of our Lord 1472 but every year thereafter. Every firstborn Weaver girl will be gifted as fair comeuppance to the firstborn Hawk boy to be claimed between the years of one and eight and six and twenty respectively. Both parties will be forever agreed on this day set forth.

The life and all attributes will be determined by the current Hawk, no rules or precedence will be set, and this agreement raises them above the law, operating within the grace of the royal decree.

Signed:

Bennett Hawk & Family

Percy Weaver & Family

Jethro

I KNEW WHEN she'd read it.

I knew when the final sentence sank in.

We had a document signed, sealed, and delivered by the royal magistrate of England giving us carte blanche to do as we liked. There was nothing illegal about my actions. There was nothing anyone could find me guilty of.

It was the ultimate approval.

Not to mention, we had wealth to ensure no one would contest it. There was nothing to fight against. The sooner she accepted that, the easier this would be.

Nila's eyes bugged wide, looking up from the parchment.

Grabbing her shoulders, I backed her against the table. The horror living in her black gaze was enough to drag a tiny bit of humanness from my cold soul.

Watching her being tasted—I wouldn't deny—it fucked me off. She was *my* plaything. *Mine* to torment.

I was pissed at my father for permitting the entire brotherhood to use her. They weren't deserving of drinking someone's misery. That right was a Hawk's and only a fucking Hawk's. Excluding my younger cock of a brother.

He deserved shit.

Grinding my teeth, I placed my palm against her sternum, pressing her breakable chest. Her heart beat like a war drum beneath my fingers.

Her lips parted, but she didn't fight as I pushed her backward.

I didn't say a word—controlling her by sheer anger and will.

Her defined stomach muscles clenched as she gave in, sprawling backward onto the table. A small sound of pain came from her lips, catching her weight on her elbows.

She refused to lie down.

She would.

My cock fucking bruised itself, punching my belt time and time again. Only I knew how she tasted when she *wanted* to be tasted. Only I knew how she sounded when she wanted it so fucking bad. And only I knew how tight she was.

That tightness belonged to me.

I doubted I'd fit. I doubted I'd get half my dick inside her, but until I'd had the pleasure of trying, no one else was permitted near her. I had the scroll giving me power over everyone on that subject—including my father.

I swallowed hard. The anger watching my brother stick his fucking tongue inside her boiled. I teetered on a dangerous edge.

Pull back.

I couldn't.

I wanted what I wanted, and I'd take what was owed to me.

"You finally understand." My voice was thicker, deeper, overrun with the dark lust that'd been created this morning. She'd done this to me. It was her curse to fix me.

I couldn't look at her without feeling her thrust against my finger. I couldn't see past the challenge. The building strength in her skinny frame.

She was learning.

I was learning.

We were learning how to play this game together.

She shivered as I dragged my hand down her front,

moving lower and lower. My cock ached for the wet temptation belonging to me. I was responsible for her.

She'd been through a lot. She'd obeyed even though she'd fought. She'd kept it together but now she was precariously close to losing it. I wasn't so heartless to ignore that craving in her eyes. The borderline insanity of needing a release. Combined with finally seeing proof that *we* were the good guys? Well, I owed her.

Just a little.

It was my job to take her to the edge, dangle her for a time, but then draw her back into safety. My purpose was to bridle everything she was, so she would do anything I asked.

Glaring into her eyes, I said, "You are mine. I am not your master or owner or boss. I am the man who controls your entire existence until you pay off your family's debts. You don't breathe unless I permit it. You don't move unless I request it. You live a simple life now. One with a single word you need remember...yes."

My touch skated from her belly to her hips.

She stiffened to a plank. Her gaze left mine, locking on the ornate ceiling.

"Look at me." My voice turned harsh, barbaric beneath its cultured refinement. "Has it sunk in yet? That I can do anything I want to you?"

She didn't respond—just like she'd been told not to. Silence. Blissful, blessed silence. She couldn't admonish or argue. She was pliant. Wondrously pliant.

She deserves a reward.

I tried to hold back.

I didn't want an audience.

But fuck it.

Shoving her higher on the table, I slapped away her position on her elbows, crashing her spine onto the wood. She cried out, then sucked in a harsh breath.

I grabbed her legs, forcing them wide.

Her pink flesh invited me, glistening, not from other

men's tongues, but arousal. Arousal for me. Arousal that I intended to take advantage of.

Grabbing an untouched glass of water from a Diamond brother, I dumped the liquid all over Nila's pussy.

She cried out; legs trying to scissor. But I didn't let her move.

The water trickled through her dark hair, pooling beneath her. It wasn't enough, but it washed at least some of the men's spit away.

I only wanted to taste her.

Hooking my hands beneath her hips, I held her tight.

"No. Don't—"

Too fucking late.

With a fleeting smile, I captured her swollen cunt in my mouth.

The moment my tongue shot out, pressing firm and hard, she arched off the table.

"Ah!" Her mouth hung wide, her neck straining as every muscle shot into stark relief. Her black hair fanned out on the table, sliding against her shoulders as she writhed on the wood.

Snapping my fingers, I glared at two Diamond brothers. They leapt to attention, grabbing her wrists and holding her down.

She squirmed. She fought. But my fingers only bit harder into her arse, keeping her pinned wide and open.

My fucking brother didn't have the right to tongue-fuck her.

But I did.

I hadn't planned on giving her such a reward, but...it wasn't just her getting off on this.

The power. The submission. Her taste. Her damn fucking taste.

I showed too much. I let go of my tight restraint and drank.

She groaned as I shifted a hand, holding her hipbones hard on the table. Then she whimpered. My tongue became my weapon of choice as I licked downward. No hesitation. No teasing.

I was there for one goal.

Her goal.

My eyes rolled back as I plunged my tongue inside her tight hot warmth.

Fuck me.

"God!" Her hips tried to run from my invasion. Her mouth opened wide; her ribcage visible as her lungs strained to breathe.

I set a pace no one would be able to ignore.

I fucked her. There was no other word for how I drove my tongue in and out, fast and possessive. The muscles in her belly clenched. She panted, she moaned, then she screamed.

She gave up the fight, giving into me.

A spasm of pre-cum dampened my jeans as her hips shot upward, her clit brushing against my nose.

Her body twisted, trying to get her hands free, but the brothers wouldn't let her go.

She turned wild. Seeking. Demanding. The same sexual creature from the stables.

I couldn't breathe without dragging her scent into my lungs. I couldn't swallow without drinking her. And I couldn't fucking think without wanting to tear off my jeans and plunge deep inside her.

My tongue worked faster, the tips of my teeth gracing her pussy as I drove deeper than I'd ever gone before.

I ate her. I fucked her. I *owned* her.

Her tight pussy squeezed my tongue, begging for more.

I'll give you more.

I'd given her too much already.

Fuck.

Her legs suddenly latched around my ears, grinding herself onto my face.

She moaned hard; a breathless beg on her lips. I couldn't stop myself.

My tongue drove harder; my head bobbed faster.
She unravelled.
She combusted.
She screamed as she came on my tongue.

Nila

OH, MY GOD.

Oh, my *God*.

It didn't. It couldn't. He didn't. I couldn't.

What the *hell* did I just do?

Jethro stood straight, breathing hard. His eyes were tight; his mouth drenched and red.

My cheeks flamed, heart racing like I'd run ten kilometres. What *was* that?

What magic did he possess that made me throw away self-consciousness, decorum, and hatred? How could I squirm that way? Sound that way? *Come* that way?

I came.

He made me come.

My captor shot me free for one blissful second, granting me something no one else had. The sparks and waves and mind-twisting delicious clenching. I wanted more. I wanted it *now*.

Jethro wiped his mouth, trying unsuccessfully to hide the lust glowing in his eyes. He'd given, not taken. He'd done what he said.

I'll wipe it all away.

The only thing I could focus on was him. The room of men didn't matter. Their tongues and touches and pleasantly whispered thank yous were gone. Burned to a crisp thanks to the nuclear explosion he'd set off. I was no longer at the mercy of the room. I *owned* the room.

Then everything came crashing back.

My first orgasm was given by a man whose father killed my mother.

My privacy had been completely stripped by the man who'd stolen me from my family.

He'd made me sleep with dogs.

He played with my head.

He didn't give a damn about me.

Why was he so clever? So perfectly designed for this game?

I struggled to sit up. The two men holding my wrists let me go, and I shot into a sitting position, wrapping arms around my torso.

The hot sparkly burst that made everything so inconsequential faded with every rapid heartbeat. It was like being in the eye of the storm. Jethro granted me silence. He'd shared his heavenly silence and quieted my mind from everything I was feeling.

But now the storm gathered strength, howling, twisting, sucking me back up the funnel of horrors.

Eyes.

So many eyes upon me. Paintings and real. Men who'd seen me naked. Men who'd licked every inch. Men who didn't care if I lived or died.

You let him control you.
You let your body rule your mind.
You let yourself down.

Crushing grief swamped me. I couldn't be there another moment. I couldn't sit there with residual sparks shivering in my core. I couldn't pretend that everything was acceptable.

Jethro smirked, his breathing calmed as he dragged large hands through his hair. My heart broke into shards. How could he give me something so incredible all while hating me? His mercurial moods, his unreadable face—it confused me. Even worse, it *upset* me.

Visceral repulsion and horror howled through me as the storm grew in strength. The compliant prisoner disappeared under a tsunami of rage. This wasn't okay. None of this was okay.

This is not okay!

Balling my hands, I scooted off the table. Keeping my distance from Jethro, I bared my teeth at him—the first male to drive me up a mountain I'd never leapt off before.

Him.

He'd had no right to make me come. To give me a gift not out of kindness but control. He'd proven a valuable lesson. He could make me do anything he wanted, and there was nothing I could do about it.

His eyebrow quirked; chin tilted with arrogance. He didn't say a word, moving to lean against the door with his hands jammed in his pockets. He gave nothing away. No hint at how he felt watching other men use me. No clue as to what he was thinking when he made me come.

I was his to repay this horrible ludicrous debt. But he didn't seem to care.

And that was what broke my heart.

He didn't give an arse about what happened to me. Everything I'd hoped—the secret plan to make him care—was smashed to dust. There was no pleasing a rock like him. No appealing to his compassion.

He has none.

Tearing my eyes from his, I glowered at the table. Standing tall, I embraced my nakedness. I throbbed with righteousness. I trembled with indecency.

I hated what I wore. It covered nothing and was theirs. I wanted nothing to do with them. I wanted to refuse their food, spit out their water, and burn their clothes. Not that they'd offered me any.

With suddenly steady hands, I tore the French maid's cap

off my head. I threw it down the table. The satin wood let it slide all the way to the centre where it rested like a stain, a sin—a simple innocuous thing screaming of wrongness.

The men didn't move.

Fumbling at the ties around my neck, I pulled the hated pinafore over my head and balled it up. Standing proud, naked—showing off my bruises from vertigo and tongue smears from bastards—I spoke. "Look at you. Look at how masculine and powerful you are." Pointing my finger around the table, I growled, "Look at how scary and dominating and strong you are. Look at how *proud* you must be. You proved you're invincible by taking advantage of a woman brought here against her will. You used a girl who has to live her worst nightmares to protect those she loves."

Stabbing myself in the chest, I whispered, "Wait…I got it wrong. *You're* not the strong ones. *I* am. You're weak and disgusting. By doing what you did, you gave me more power than I've ever had before. You gave me a new skill—a skill at ignoring you because you're nothing. Nothing. *Nothing*!"

"And you!" I swung my arm, gaze zeroing in on Jethro. The one man who held my life in the palm of his hand. He was nothing. Just like his brethren of bastards.

Jethro stood taller, a shadow darkening his face. His hands came out of his pockets, crossing in front of his large chest.

"You…" I seethed. "You think you're the baddest one here. You think I'll cower. You think I'll obey." Running both hands through my hair, I shouted, "I'll *never* cower. I'll *never* obey. You'll never break me, because you can't touch me."

Spanning my arms, I presented my naked form as a gift—the gift he'd hinted at wanting but hadn't taken. "I'll never be yours even though you own my life. I'll never bow to you because my knees don't recognise your so-called power. So do your worst. Hurt me. Rape me. Kill me. But you'll never ever own me."

Breathing hard, I waited.

The room had remained silent. But now it filled with

rustling of leather as men shifted in their seats. The atmosphere went from shocked silence to heavy anticipation.

My overworked heart kicked into another gear, sending my vision a little grey, a little fuzzy. *Please, not now.*

Planting my legs, gripping the soft carpet beneath my toes, I locked my knees against a wave of vertigo.

Mr. Hawk was the first to move. He placed his elbows on the table, linking his fingers together. "I was wrong. You're nothing like your mother. She had a brain. She was smart." His voice dropped the chivalrous country man edge, deepening into violent snaps, "You, on the other hand, are wilful and stupid. You don't see that *we* are your family now. The moment you slept under my roof you became a Hawk by means of acquisition."

I laughed. "I'm still a Weaver then because I didn't sleep under your roof." My kitten claws sharpened. I'd never been a fighter, but something called to me. Something intoxicating and lethal.

He leaned forward, anger etching his face. "You *will* learn your place. Mark my words."

I wanted to fight. I'd listened to their damn history lessons, it was time they listened to mine. "I may not have records so perfectly kept as yours, but I do know my family is innocent. Whatever happened back then was between them—not us. Leave it in the past. My family created a business of making clothes. We dressed the royal court but also donated to the poor. I'm proud of where I've come from and for you to—"

"Jet!" Mr. Hawk pinched the bridge of his nose. "Shut her up."

Jethro immediately slammed a hand over my mouth.

I froze. I knew I'd brought whatever punishment was about to happen upon myself. I couldn't blame anyone, but I wouldn't let myself regret what I'd said. I believed I was a good person. So were my twin, father, mother, and ancestors.

"You just had to push," Jethro hissed. "I'm going to draw

blood for this."

My heart rabbited but I forced myself to remember one important fact.

They can't hurt you too much.

There would be pain. There would be agony. But they meant to keep me alive. I had debts to repay before my life was stolen.

Never taking his eyes off mine, Mr. Hawk, ordered, "Jethro. Teach this woman that Hawks are a forgiving family but there are times when strictness is required in lieu of allowing little tantrums like this to occur." His eyes switched from mine to his son's. "Take her. Deal with her. I don't want to see her again until she's lost the misplaced righteousness she seems to think she's owed."

Jethro nodded, jostling our bodies. His fingers unglued from around my mouth and he grabbed my wrist. Every part of me shrank from his overbearing body and granite golden eyes, but I forced myself to stand tall.

I growled, "Whatever you do won't matter. What happened before will *never* happen again." I would never let my body rule my mind no matter what he did. "You may be able to hurt me but you should know how pathetic it is for a man to hurt a woman. That isn't power. It's a weakness!"

He grunted under his breath. "Motherfucking Christ." His temper increased until the large room pulsed with it.

Another wave of vertigo grabbed my brain. But I managed the impossible, fighting through the grey unsteady wave—staying on my feet.

I fought the imbalance thanks to letting myself unlock so many facets of who I truly was. I stood proud and naked, wearing only dried saliva and bruises.

Jethro jerked me closer. He swallowed his anger until nothing outward showed—no annoyance or amazement—he was as opaque as a black iceberg and just as sharp.

"If you will, Ms. Weaver." Suddenly he let me go, waving toward the double doors behind me. They opened wide as if staff waited on the other side for his command.

When I didn't move, he snapped, "Now!"

My arms wanted to wind around my body. I wanted to hide from his intense gaze, but I fought every instinct and elegantly pirouetted on my toes. I left the room as demurely and proudly as possible. Without a backward glance.

The moment the doors slammed behind us, Jethro grabbed my elbow, prowling forward as if the flames of hell craved his soul. I went from walking to jogging to keep up with his pace.

My vision lost its clarity for a moment, fading in and out as another wash of unbalance tried to steal me, but Jethro didn't give me time to give in. He didn't give me time to care that he dragged me down a corridor so wide it could've been a hall. He didn't let me inspect the countless weapons—swords, bayonets, crossbows, and knives—or catch the eye of surprised staff.

I breathed hard when we finally crashed through one of the many exterior doors and were welcomed from brooding red corridor to bright early-autumn sun.

Jethro kept walking, not letting me catch my breath.

Dragging me down the four huge steps, I winced as the gravel bit into the soles of my feet. But he didn't care. He didn't even notice.

Our feet kicked up pebbles as he headed toward the treeline several metres from the house. I'd never seen this side of the property before. But the grounds were just as expansive and impressive as the other perimeters and just as dangerous.

This was my cage. Leaves and thorns and brambles.

And I'm naked.

The moment gravel was replaced by soft grass below my toes, Jethro tossed me away. I would've fallen if I wasn't malleable and given up fighting his momentum. I stumbled forward, arms soaring outward as if I could suddenly leave the world behind and fly. Fly away. Fly free.

The moment I came to a halt, I spun to face him.

Jethro was right behind me. He fisted my hair, twisting my neck.

I whimpered as he raised my head, higher and higher. My eyes coasted over his crisp grey shirt, and locked onto a pair of ferocious eyes.

"Tell me. What did you hope to achieve in there?" He didn't give me a chance to reply, tugging my hair in a painful jerk. "Did you honestly think before you opened your mouth? If you had stood there and been silent, it would've all been over. You earned an afternoon on your own in a hot steam bath. A maid to bring you whatever you wanted to eat." He shook me. "What part of a *gift* for good behaviour did you not understand?"

"I don't want your charity."

He groaned. "It's not fucking charity if you've earned it." Lowering his head, his nose pressed against mine.

I froze.

"You earned it today. You pleased me by letting those men sample you. You surprised me in a good way." The softness of his voice disappeared under a torrent of rage. "But then you fucked it all up by being *you*. And now…" He trailed off, ideas glowing in his eyes.

Letting me go, I backed away from him, grabbing my hair and quickly twisting it into a loose braid down my back. I hated the thickness, the length. It seemed to invite Jethro to use it anyway he pleased. My scalp had never been so bruised.

The diamond collar sent little rainbows of light bouncing from the sunlight. I would've laughed if I wasn't so tense. I was naked but wearing rainbows—I never would've thought to combine magic with fashion.

Ideas for a new design line came thick and fast. I craved a pencil to sketch before they disappeared.

Jethro placed both hands on his hips, watching me silently.

I didn't move. I didn't say a word. The fragile ceasefire between us stretched uncomfortably thin. It would either snap and ricochet onto me with terrible pain or fade away like a feather on a breeze.

"I see threats don't work on you. But perhaps a negotiation might."

Despite myself, curiosity and hope swelled in my heart. "A negotiation?"

"A one shot offer. You win, you're free. I win, you forget about your old life and give in. You say I'll never own you. If I win—you willingly give me that right." His lips pulled into a cold smile. "You sign not only the debt agreement but another—one that makes me your master until your last breath is taken. You do that, and I'll give you this."

"Give me what?" I asked breathlessly.

"A chance at freedom."

My eyes popped wide.

What?

He cocked his head at the forest behind me. "You wanted to be free—so go. Run. Go seek your freedom."

I twisted on the spot, looking over my shoulder. The sun dappled patches of leaf-strewn ground, looking like a fairy glen, but then it grew darker and thicker and scarier.

The diamond collar rested heavy and ruinously ominous on my throat. My spine ached from the short time I'd been made to wear it; the coldness still hadn't adapted to my skin. How could I run with such a deterrent?

How can you not?

It was the one chance I'd hoped for. The one chance I didn't think I'd get.

Squeezing my eyes, I let Jethro's ultimatum—his negotiation—seep into my brain. If I ran, I might make it. If I ran, I might get what I wanted. But if I lost...

Turning to face him again, the golden-light from the sun cast him with ghostly silhouette, blurring his outline, creating more than just a man. He looked as if he had one foot in this world and one in hell. A fallen angel who still burned with fire—yet it wasn't purity he burned with but hate.

Jethro raised an eyebrow. "What's it going to be?"

"I don't know what you're offering."

"Yes you do."

I did. *I do.*

He took a small step toward me. "You want to break the contract? You want to keep your brother and father safe? Fine. I'm giving you a one-time deal. Run. If you make it to the boundary, you're free. Your family will never be hunted by the Hawks again. You make it, and this is all over. Every last debt and ounce of history—disappears." His voice licked through the sunshine.

A small sparkle from my earlier orgasm rippled between my legs. "And if I don't?"

Jethro frowned. "What?"

"If I don't run…what happens then?"

"You wouldn't run? After I just offered you what you've wanted all along?"

I crossed my wrists over the junction of my thighs, hiding my pussy. "I didn't say I wanted the chance to run naked through a thousand hectares. I said I wanted this to be over."

Jethro smirked. "It's not over until it's over." His eyes fell to my collar, glinting with darkness. "And we both know how it will be over."

Moving closer, he said quietly, "There is no other option here, Ms. Weaver. I'm not giving you the choice to run. I'm *telling* you to run. You wanted it. You got it. One chance to save your family as well as your own life. One chance. You do not want to fuck it up by testing my patience."

My mind stumbled with everything that'd happened. There was no denying chemistry flew between us—but Jethro didn't respond. He was only interested in the chase. The hunt. The *sport.*

He stood so close, every time he breathed, his chest almost touched my nipples. He didn't seem to care I was naked or offer clothing for this one and only chance at freedom. He would make me run unprotected through a forest full of brambles, predators, and trip-worthy roots.

His arm raised and I clamped every muscle from cringing as he cupped my cheek. His heady scent of woods and leather settled over me. Tracing the pad of his thumb over my cheekbone, he bowed his head. "Run, Ms. Weaver. Run. But one thing you should know before you go."

Do not play his games. Do not rise to the bait.

My lips stayed pinched together. I stiffened in his hold.

His mouth tickled the soft skin below my ear. "While you're running, I'll be hunting. You not only have to get to the boundary but you have to do it before I catch you."

The tingle and horrible promise of hope evaporated. Cruel. Vicious. Evil.

I'm to be hunted.

There wouldn't be freedom. There would only be blood. Just like he said in the dining room.

Energy left my limbs. Who was I kidding? I hadn't eaten since I was stolen. I'd barely had a decent sleep. I existed like a junkie on adrenaline and fear. It was no combination for a long distance run through thickets and bush.

Jethro pulled away, dropping his hands. He smiled. "Your head start begins now, Ms. Weaver. I'd leave if I were you."

Now?

I backpeddled, heart bursting with terror. "How—how long do I have?"

Jethro carefully raised his cuff, looking sedately at the diamond and black watch on his wrist. "I'm a seasoned hunter. I have no doubt I'll find you. And when I do…what those men did to you will be nothing." Cocking his head, he said, "I think forty-five minutes is rather sporting, don't you?"

My mind was no longer there. It was leaping and flying over leaves and dodging ancient trunks.

Run. Go. Run.

"Make it and you're no longer mine…."

Freedom taunted me, making me believe I had a chance. A slim, barely non-existent chance—but still a chance. The muscles in my legs reacted, already poised to take off. I had to trust my body. It knew how to flee.

I could make it. If I did, I would no longer be his pet to torture. But if I didn't....

Don't ask. Don't ask.

"And if I don't?"

Jethro lowered his head, glaring at me beneath his brow. His eyes were tight and dark, glinting with excitement at the upcoming hunt. "Don't and the debt I'll make you repay will make you wish you *had* made it to the boundary." He stepped from the sun's glare, his teeth sparkling like diamonds. "Now...run."

...

...

I ran.

Continues in FIRST DEBT

"You say I'll never own you. If I win—you willingly give me that right. You sign not only the debt agreement, but another—one that makes me your master until your last breath is taken. You do that, and I'll give you this."

Nila Weaver's family is indebted. Stolen, taken, and bound not by monsters but by an agreement written over six hundred years ago, she has no way out.

She belongs to Jethro as much as she denies it.

Jethro Hawk's patience is running out. His inheritance gift tests, challenges, and surprises him—and not in good ways. He hasn't leashed her but he thinks he might've found a way to bind her forever.

Debts are mounting. Payment waiting.

<u>THE ENTIRE SERIES IN THE INDEBTED SERIES ARE OUT NOW!</u>

About the Author

Pepper Winters is a New York Times, Wall Street Journal, and USA Today International Bestseller. She loves dark romance, star-crossed lovers, and the forbidden taboo. She strives to write a story that makes the reader crave what they shouldn't, and delivers tales with complex plots and unforgettable characters.

After chasing her dreams to become a full-time writer, Pepper has earned recognition with awards for best Dark Romance, best BDSM Series, and best Dark Hero. She's an #1 iBooks bestseller, along with #1 in Erotic Romance, Romantic Suspense, Contemporary, and Erotica Thriller. She's also honoured to wear the IndieReader Badge for being a Top 10 Indie Bestseller, and recently signed a two book deal with Hachette. Represented by Trident Media, her books have garnered foreign and audio interest and are currently being translated into numerous languages. They will be in available in bookstores worldwide.

Her Dark Romance books include (click for buylinks):
Tears of Tess (Monsters in the Dark #1)
Quintessentially Q (Monsters in the Dark #2)
Twisted Together (Monsters in the Dark #3)
Debt Inheritance (Indebted #1)

First Debt (Indebted Series #2)
Second Debt (Indebted Series #3)
Third Debt (Indebted Series #4)
Fourth Debt (Indebted Series #5)
Final Debt (Indebted Series #6)

Her Grey Romance books include (click for buylinks):
Destroyed
Ruin & Rule (Pure Corruption MC #1)

Upcoming releases are (click the link to add to Goodreads)
Sin & Suffer (Pure Corruption #2)
Je Suis a Toi (Monsters in the Dark Novella)
Unseen Messages (Contemporary Survival Romance)
Super Secret Series to be announced early 2016

To be the first to know of upcoming releases, please join Pepper's Newsletter (she promises never to spam or annoy you.)

Pepper's Newsletter

Or follow her on her website
Pepper Winters

You can stalk her here:
Pinterest
Facebook Pepper Winters
Twitter
Website
Facebook Group
Goodreads

She loves mail of any kind: pepperwinters@gmail.com

Other Books by Pepper

Tears of Tess (Monsters in the Dark #1)
"My life was complete. Happy, content, everything neat and perfect.
Then it all changed.
I was sold."
Buy Now

Quintessentially Q (Monsters in the Dark #2)
"All my life, I battled with the knowledge I was twisted… screwed up to want something so deliciously dark—wrong on so many levels. But then slave fifty-eight entered my world. Hissing, fighting, with a core of iron, she showed me an existence where two wrongs do make a right."
Buy Now

Twisted Together (Monsters in the Dark #3)
"After battling through hell, I brought my esclave back from the brink of ruin. I sacrificed everything—my heart, my mind, my very desires to bring her back to life. And for a while, I thought it broke me, that I'd never be the same. But slowly the beast is growing bolder, and it's finally time to show Tess how beautiful the dark can be."
Buy Now

Destroyed (Standalone Grey Romance)
She has a secret.
He has a secret.
One secret destroys them.
Buy Now

Ruin & Rule (Pure Corruption MC #1)
"We met in a nightmare. The in-between world where time had no power over reason. We fell in love. We fell hard. But then we woke up. And it was over . . ."
Buy Now

Unseen Messages
"I should've listened, should've paid attention. The messages were there. Warning me. But I didn't see and I paid the price..."
Buy Now

All other titles and updates can be found on her **Goodreads Page.**

Playlist

Leave out the rest by Linkin Park
In the end by Linkin Park
Yesterday by Fallout Boy
Butterflies and Hurricanes by Muse
Breath of Life by Florence and the Machine
The Lonely by Christina Perri
Titanium by David Guetta
Bittersweet Symphony by The Verve
Battlecry by Imagine Dragons
I know what you did in the dark by Fallout Boys
Copy of A by Nine Inch Nails
Strange Love by Depeche Mode
Precious by Depeche Mode
Louder by Lea Michele

Acknowledgements

Thank you so much to: Jenny from Editing4Indies and Kayla The Bibliophile for doing an amazing editing job and squeezing me in late notice.

Thanks to my amazing beta readers: Kristi, Mandi, Melissa, Skye, Ker, Kiki, Tamicka, and Yaya. Your incredible feedback made this book shine.

Thanks to the incredible duo who I adore, Aussie Lisa and NinaAfterDark. I don't know what I would've done without your support and you reading the first edition of Jethro and Nila.

Thanks so much to Rachel, Skye, Lyra, Lili, and too many other amazing people to mention who talk to me on a daily basis, share their ups and downs, and make me feel less insane as a writer.

Thanks to Nadine for running my street team and being such a huge supporter.

Thank you so much to the amazing Ari from Cover it Designs for my kick ass covers. I can't wait to reveal the remaining ones for this series.

Thank you to The Rock Stars of Romance for hosting the review and blog tour. You guys had to put up with me in many ways so I'm very grateful.

Thank you to Love Between the Sheets for putting up with my nightmarish double bookings and lack of coordination.

Thank you to my readers who just make me feel so loved and appreciated in all things that I write.

Thank you to hubby for cooking me dinner, keeping me alive, and overlooking the fact I now work entirely in pyjamas.

And finally, thank you universe for making my dreams come true.

Thank you so much for Reading

xxx

Printed in Great Britain
by Amazon